Close to Her Heart

A Carrigans of the Circle C Novel

C.J. Carmichael

TULE
PUBLISHING

Dedication

For the one-and-only Jane Porter. Thank you for being one of my best friends and writing pals—and for supporting my Carrigans of the Circle C novels.

Carrigans of the Circle C

Promise Me, Cowboy (novella)
Good Together (novel)
Close To Her Heart (novel)
Snowbound in Montana (novella)
A Cowgirl's Christmas (novel)

April

WHEN THE ULTRASOUND technician excused herself from the examining room, Dani Carrigan was unconcerned. As a healthy, thirty-four-year-old woman, with no family history of relevant medical problems, she didn't see the need.

She had other matters on her mind.

First, the need to urinate. She'd been instructed to drink several glasses of water prior to the ultrasound.

Plus, her exposed belly was cold, thanks to the gel the technician had gooped over her skin. The gel had been warm when the technician—an intensely serious woman about Dani's age who had introduced herself as Emily—first applied it. But it had cooled now, and the air circulating from the heating system at the University of Washington Medical Clinic didn't help.

Dani glanced at the empty chair next to her examining table. Most women these days brought their husband, or significant other with them to these things.

Her significant other still didn't know she was pregnant.

She had to tell him soon.

Her belly had popped two weeks ago, and for that amount of time she'd been avoiding sex. But her last reason

1

not to invite him back to her place after they'd gone out for a nice dinner—she had too much paperwork to catch up on— had caused him to raise his eyebrows. She'd never used work as an excuse before.

Dani closed her eyes, picturing Adrian Carlson in her mind. She loved his thick, slightly wavy dark hair, which he wore short at the sides, but piled high over a forehead with a slight widow's peak. He had intense gray eyes, deep set under serious eyebrows. Strong cheekbones, a firm jaw. And a mouth that often quirked up at one corner, when he was amused.

More importantly, he was the most intelligent man she'd ever met. And he was also the Department Head of Psychology. In other words—her boss.

If that wasn't complicated enough, he already had a child. A daughter, Ava, who was only six years old. The mother—his wife—had died two years ago. Adrian was very protective of his daughter. So much so, Dani still hadn't met her, even though she was anxious to do so. Dani knew how painful it was to lose a mother prematurely and she felt that she would be able to offer some comfort to the little girl.

In time, Adrian always said when she raised the subject.

Dani was very much afraid that Adrian wasn't going to welcome the news that she was pregnant. But maybe he would surprise her. Perhaps a new child would be just the sort of life-altering event that would make him finally ready to commit fully to their relationship. Including—and this was a long shot, and maybe old-fashioned of her to even want, but she did—marriage.

The door to the examining room opened, letting in a waft of air that chilled her belly further, as well as the technician and a second medical professional—this one a man in his forties with a white lab coat, wearing wire glasses that had slid partly down his very narrow and long nose.

"Dani? I'm Dr. Buttress. I'm just going to have a look at these pictures." He took the wand and began running it over her belly, just as the technician had already done. He began by scanning all over, and then narrowed in on a certain small area.

Dani felt the first sliver of concern.

She'd seen the beating heart. She knew her baby was alive.

"Is something wrong?" Up until now, every one of her doctor appointments had been completely normal. Her OB, Dr. Gwen Fong, was relaxed and reassuring. "Keep doing what you're doing, Dani. Continue with those iron and folate supplements, and remember to take some time to exercise moderately, every day."

Earlier, when the technician had asked if she wanted to know the sex of the baby, Dani had been tempted. Girl? Or boy?

Having grown up with three sisters, she'd be so much more comfortable with a girl. But maybe Adrian would prefer a son? She felt sexist and uncomfortable even entertaining that thought.

But now, the baby's sex was the furthest thing from her mind.

Just let her—or him—be healthy.

Please.

When she'd first figured out she was pregnant, Dani had been surprised by her strong emotional reaction. It had gone beyond happiness, had been, in fact, the purest sensation of joy that she'd ever experienced.

Dani was a scientist, a PhD in psychology accustomed to making logical decisions based on the facts of a situation.

In her case, having a baby didn't make sense. She had a demanding career that she loved. She wasn't married. Had no family living in Seattle for support.

Yet. She desperately wanted this baby. At night when she put her hands on her belly and closed her eyes, she imagined holding a newborn in her arms. Breastfeeding, then rocking her to sleep. She'd held her sister Mattie's twin daughters when they were little and remembered how light and delicate they had seemed.

So precious.

Dani focused on Dr. Buttress's milky brown eyes, trying to glean a hint of what was going on in his head. He relinquished the wand, peered once more at the screen, then stood back on his heels.

"The heart looks good. Baby's size is what we'd expect at sixteen weeks…"

She could sense the "but." She held her breath as she waited for it.

"But I'm seeing a few markers here." He glanced away from her, back at the screen.

Dani's gaze flew to the technician. Emily's lips were pressed together in a sympathetic expression. Far from reassured, Dani turned back to the doctor.

"High fluid levels at the nuchal translucency." He pointed on the screen to a spot on the baby's neck. "Also the little finger only has two joints and the femurs are short relative to body size."

Dani reflexively bent her only little finger, noting the way she could curl it into her palm. Only two joints—that didn't seem too bad. And if the baby was on the short side, well, that was okay, too. She and Sage were tall, but their other two sisters—Mattie and Callan—could definitely be classified as petite.

The doctor sighed. "We can't be sure. Not from just one ultrasound. But these are markers for Down Syndrome."

ॐ ॐ

DANI STEPPED OUT the main doors of the Medical Center, managed a few steps, before freezing in confusion. Where had she parked her car?

She glanced around, taking stock of her surroundings. She noticed the deep blue of the afternoon sky, the fresh green of the grass, the shy pink of cherry blossoms only just past their prime. Seattle was at its best in April, though the city was pretty all year round, with a mild climate so unlike the harsh winters and scorching summers of Montana.

Homesickness hit her with a punch of aching sadness. If only she could be in the kitchen of the Circle C ranch, with all her sisters at the table doing homework or just gabbing, and Mom busy at one of her usual spots by the sink or the stove. Dani longed to be a child again, with few responsibilities and no difficult decisions expected of her.

But, she was an adult. And her mom had been dead for a long time.

Suddenly, she remembered where she'd left the car.

As she strode toward it—a semblance of the confident, professional woman who'd shown up for this appointment—she thought about how she'd expected this day to end.

She'd booked the ultrasound for late on a Friday afternoon, so she could go straight home afterward. The plan had been to spend the weekend spreading the news. First, her sisters, starting with Sage, who was as sweet as the chocolates she made for the townspeople of Marietta, Montana. No matter what she really thought of Dani being pregnant, Sage would react with only kindness and joy.

Dani would call Mattie, next, on her ranch just south of Flathead Lake. Since Mattie had daughters of her own—one of whom, Portia, was enrolled in university here in Seattle, taking Dani's Intro to Psych class—she would be excited as well.

Youngest sister Callan, still at home with their father on the Circle C, was more of a wild card. She might be thrilled, indifferent or disapproving, depending on her mood.

Dani's father, Hawksley, however, was sure to be unimpressed. But that didn't matter. He'd never been very involved in any of their lives. Since their mother's death, when Dani was sixteen, he'd been even more removed.

Dani negotiated her Volvo through the early-rush-hour traffic, relieved when she finally pulled into the parking space under the condo building she'd lived in for the past two years. She gathered her purse and briefcase, anxious for the moment when she could kick off her heels, put on some comfy clothes and pour herself a glass of—Four months ago she would have enjoyed a glass of white wine. These days, her beverage of choice was usually milk.

After that, Dani wasn't sure what she'd do. Certainly, she wouldn't be making those phone calls she'd planned. Not after that awful ultrasound. No, tonight she just wanted to be alone and have a chance to regroup. When she was stronger, maybe after dinner, she'd get on the web and do some research.

Down Syndrome.

The words hovered in her mind like an unwanted guest she wished she'd seen coming so she could have refused to open the door. She had more than a layman's knowledge of the syndrome, as it was included in materials in one of her courses. She also remembered a girl who'd been a year younger than her in grade school, a girl who had often played alone during recess. The girl had been short, somewhat clumsy, with small slanted eyes, thick glasses, and a tendency to stare down at her feet when she was walking.

Was her baby going to be like that girl?

Dani blinked as tears suddenly blurred her vision. Not wanting to risk being trapped with a stranger on the elevator—or worse, one of her friends—she took the stairs to the eighth floor of her building. There were six, three-bedroom units here, but only the four on the west side—including hers—had city and ocean views.

Her hand was on the doorknob, she'd actually inserted

her key, when Eliot emerged from the door beside hers. Damn. Eliot was the last person she wanted to run into right now.

"Hey, stranger," he said easily. "You're home early for a work day."

She forced a smile before looking at him. "Slacking off. You caught me."

He must have come home from work early, too, because he'd already changed from his usual suit into the sort of weekend casual clothes one would expect to see in a Ralph Lauren ad: dark jeans, a vaguely nautical navy sweater with thin white stripes across the chest, and loafers that probably cost more than a pair of tickets to the Mariners.

Was it her imagination, or was Eliot checking out her waistline?

"I was talking to Miriam earlier. We're thinking tonight would be good for a Happy Hour party. My place," he added.

Miriam also lived on this floor. The three of them had evolved into friends over the two years they'd lived here, shortly after the renovated condo units were put on the market and promptly snapped up by upwardly mobile professionals. Their Happy Hour parties lay at the crux of that friendship, but she'd been avoiding them since she'd found out she was pregnant. "Well…"

"You better not suggest we have brunch on Sunday, instead. You've used that line too many times this winter."

True. Because she could avoid drinking alcohol for brunch. If she turned down a drink at one of their Happy

Hour parties—which involved imbibing copious amounts of a feature cocktail, chosen and supplied by the host of the evening, followed by several rounds of nerdy board games like Rumi Cube or Scrabble—they'd know right away something was up.

This was supposed to be the weekend when she came clean. After the phone calls to her family, she'd planned to tell Miriam and Eliot next. She'd been nervous about their reactions *before* she found out about the Down Syndrome markers.

Now, she was terrified.

Yet, she had to tell *someone.* She was so tired of keeping such a big secret. Of feeling run-down and nauseous without being able to complain to anyone. Of worrying about the future, about Adrian's reaction, about how she was going to handle this at the university…

She could feel tears filling her eyes again and dipped her head so Eliot wouldn't see them. But she was too late.

Eliot touched her chin, lifting her face a few inches. "I had a feeling something was wrong."

He took her briefcase out of her hand, and pushed open her door. Ushering her inside, he went straight to the fridge. "I'm going to pour you a drink and you're going to tell me everything. It's Adrian, right?"

Eliot had never met Adrian, but he didn't like him just the same. *On principle,* he often said, at which point Miriam would nod and give Dani a look. *I'm not saying anything, because girls have to stick together, but you do know Eliot is right, don't you?*

Dani sank into one of the white leather chairs next to the fireplace. She knew what Eliot was looking for. In less than a minute, he'd have it all figured out.

"You don't have an open bottle of white?" Eliot shut the fridge, then checked the cupboard where she kept her stash. When she wasn't drinking cute cocktails invented by her friends, Dani always drank white wine.

"Mother Hubbard, what's going on here? You're completely out of—"

And just like that, Eliot went silent. As it extended, Dani imagined him thinking about her avoidance tactics lately, counting back the weeks and the months, to when they'd begun. As her friend left the kitchen and settled in the chair next to hers, she braced herself.

"How long have you been pregnant?" he asked.

"Late December. I didn't figure it out until I missed my period in January, though."

He fell back into his chair, knocked there by her words. "Holy shit."

"I'm due September eighth," she added.

No mistaking the look to her belly now. Eliot glanced from her slightly thickened waistline to her face.

"How's Adrian feel about it?"

Damn. He would have to ask that. "I haven't told him. Yet. Haven't told anyone."

"So I'm the first. I'd be honored, except for the fact that I had to take inventory of your wine cellar in order to figure it out."

"The pregnancy wasn't planned. Obviously. I was afraid

to tell people until I figured out how I felt about it."

"And—?"

"I still haven't figured it out." This was a lie. She knew what she wanted. The baby. Adrian. Marriage. She wanted it all, and she'd just hoped and hoped that somehow it would work out. If just once Adrian had mentioned something about taking their relationship to the next level. Even if he'd suggested it was time she met Ava. All she'd needed was a positive sign and she would have blurted out the news, she knew she would have.

But through all of January, February and March Adrian seemed perfectly content to continue with their usual routine. Dinner at her place, once or twice a week, followed by an hour or two in bed. Adrian had a live-in-nanny for Ava, which afforded him a certain amount of flexibility with his work and social life. Occasionally, he would go so far as to fall asleep with her after they made love, or stay to watch a movie. But he'd always rouse himself before dawn, so he could hurry home before his daughter woke up.

The situation was far from ideal. But she'd known that walking in. Sleeping with the department head wasn't smart. Of course, they had to keep quiet about it. As for Adrian's devotion to Ava—would she love him as much if he wasn't such a great dad?

She sighed.

"So are you saying you might not keep this baby?" Eliot asked tentatively.

She didn't answer. Not once had she thought about termination. Not once, that was, until her ultrasound today...

Eliot got out of the chair. "Let me get you something. What do pregnant women drink? Tea?"

"I'll have a glass of milk."

He blinked. "Yes. I thought that was strange. You have a gallon of the stuff in your fridge. Not even fat free."

She put a hand on her belly. "I'm following the nutritional advice of my doctor."

"Okay. So then, you *are* keeping the baby." Eliot went to the kitchen and poured the milk.

"Yes," she said, the word coming out instinctively. In that moment, she made a decision to keep quiet about the ultrasound. It could be the doctor had made a mistake. The images were so fuzzy. She would wait until her meeting with her OB next week before jumping to any conclusions.

Just making the decision to keep quiet about that part of things made her feel calmer.

"Wow. That's, um, that's major, Dani." Eliot poured a second glass of milk.

"One will be enough," she said.

"It's for me. Seems like with news this big, I should join you in a toast." He came back to the living room with both glasses, handed her one, and then raised his own. "To a healthy baby."

She almost choked on her first swallow. Had Eliot somehow guessed? But no. Proposing a toast to a healthy baby was a completely natural thing to do. "Thank you."

"I can't remember the last time I had a glass of milk," Eliot said after his first sip. "Not bad." He was working on downing the glass, like it was a medicinal necessity, when his phone began playing the opening music from *The Good Wife*, a signal that this was a work call, probably one of his female clients.

Eliot was one of the city's top divorce attorneys, known for his ability to reach settlements without the need for courtroom drama. Dani had heard him on enough phone calls to know he had excellent behind-the-scenes negotiating abilities, and a sympathetic and charming manner with his clients. Though he claimed he hadn't intended his practice to include only female clients, somehow most of them were. His boyish good looks probably had something to do with that. Not to mention, his incredible capacity for sympathetic listening.

Though she knew Eliot was too ethical to actually get involved romantically with any of these women, the way he spoke to them, Dani was sure the majority fell at least a little in love with him.

Eliot set down the glass and pulled out his phone, speaking in his professional *you can count on me* voice. "Eliot Gilmore. Hi, Christine. How are you doing?"

Dani smirked. When he raised his eyebrows at her, she found a tissue then wiped off his milk moustache.

Eliot succumbed to the clean-up, standing perfectly still. His eyes were on hers as he spoke into the phone. "How upsetting for you," he said, sounding as if one-hundred percent of his concentration was on the woman on the other end of the conversation. Then, when Dani had finished wiping the film of milk from his upper lip, he turned, moving to the windows and the view of the Sound. "Did he really? Your husband is going to pay for that."

Once when she'd asked why Eliot had chosen to specialize in divorce law, he'd replied, in all seriousness, "We all have to follow where our talents lead us. You're good at analyzing early childhood factors that lead to academic success in later years. I'm good at helping people split up."

He was a funny guy, Eliot. He always delivered lines like that with a straight face, so she could never tell if he was poking fun, or not.

Leaving him alone to talk with his client, Dani went to her bedroom where she changed out of the slacks, blouse and jacket she'd worn to work that day, first undoing the safety pin she'd used to hold the waist band together. She had to go maternity wear shopping this weekend. Nothing was fitting anymore.

Except her yoga clothes.

She put on a pair of stretchy black capris, then a wine-colored, long-sleeved t-shirt that hugged the new curve in her tummy in a gentle, but obvious way. For a minute, she studied her profile in the full-length mirror at the back of her walk-in closet. She put a hand on the bump and told herself it was going to be okay. Her mother had delivered four healthy daughters. Her sister Mattie's twins had been perfect, too.

By the time she returned to the living room, Eliot was ending his conversation. But he hadn't yet slipped the phone back into his pocket when it started ringing again, this time with the theme music from *The Game of Thrones*, their favorite show. Which meant it was Miriam.

"Sweetie." Eliot's tone was brighter and more relaxed than the one he'd used with his client. He listened a bit then said, "I'm with her right now. Why don't you—"

Before he could finish his sentence, Dani's door was opened and Miriam walked in looking perfect, as usual, in a black skirt and lacy black top. Miriam only wore the one color—and why not?—it looked fabulous on her. She had smooth, delicate features, shiny black hair, and dark eyes fringed with thick, sooty lashes. Her parents had moved to Vancouver from Hong Kong before it reverted to Chinese control and Miriam had grown up in Canada. She'd gone to college at UW though, and claimed to have no interest in ever moving back to the northern country.

After earning her masters in English Literature, Miriam had taken on a variety of vague internet publishing jobs. Though she never shared details, Dani gathered that she designed book covers and edited manuscripts for authors of self-published books. At least once a month she went to visit her parents in Vancouver but only for a few days.

Her life plan, she'd told Dani and Eliot, was to meet someone half-way tolerable and have a Green Card wedding, so she could get her American citizenship. Miriam's definition of "half-way tolerable" was probably more like Dani's "close to perfect." Miriam was always going for first dates with men she'd vetted on various Internet dating sites. Almost never, did she go on a second.

Dani knew all about wanting to escape the place you came from. It was why she was where she was, a successful academic at one of the best universities on the West Coast. Otherwise, she'd be cleaning horse poop from stalls back in Montana.

Okay. Maybe not the fairest way to describe the work that her sisters Callan and Mattie loved so much. But still. Not for her.

"So the party is on?" Miriam asked, looking puzzled. "I thought it was going to be at your place?" She glanced at Eliot when she said this. Then her attention went from him to the half-full glass of milk still in his hand, and the second, empty but filmed glass on the counter.

"So what are we drinking tonight?"

Before either Eliot or Dani could say anything, Miriam took Eliot's glass and had a swallow.

"Ewww. What is this?"

This time Dani had no trouble getting the joke. She and Eliot both laughed so hard, neither one of them could answer for about ten seconds. Finally Dani managed to say, "m-milk," which only made Miriam frown more deeply.

"Why the hell are the two of you drinking milk?"

Eliot glanced at her, raising his eyebrows with theatrical significance. Obviously this was her news to spill. Dani took a deep breath, then splayed her hands over her tummy and turned so Miriam could see her silhouette.

"Oh. My. God." Miriam put both hands to her face.

Dani stood there, feeling self-conscious as both her friends stared at her tiny baby bump.

"So," Miriam spoke slowly. "This is why you've been avoiding us? And here I thought you were offended by my

Christmas gift."

The gift *had* been a bit of a sore spot. A T-shirt printed with the slogan: *I could be social. Or I could read. (I'm going to read.)*

Dani had wanted to protest when she opened it. "What do you mean? I'm social. Aren't I?" But she supposed by some standards, she wasn't. And she did have to admit that she had a reputation for refusing to go along on Miriam's shopping trips and Eliot's afternoon matinees when she was in the middle of a good novel.

Still, the t-shirt's indictment had hurt. Especially when Eliot had hooted with laughter after reading it.

"I haven't been avoiding *you*. I've been avoiding *alcohol*."

"There's a difference?" Eliot deadpanned.

"Exactly." He'd made her point. "Since we always drink when we get together in the evenings, what choice did I have?"

"You mean other than the truth?" Miriam shrugged one of her petite shoulders. "You could have told us you were pregnant."

Dani let out an exasperated sigh. How many people were going to be pissed with her that she hadn't shared her news sooner? Fortunately, Eliot saved her from having to respond this time.

"She needed time to process. To re-vision her life. And yes," Eliot looked up from his phone, which had captured his interest for the third time that afternoon. "She's going to keep the kid. Who happens to be due early September."

"Thank you for the brief," Miriam said.

"It's what we lawyers do best." He hesitated. "Actually, second-best—" a wolfish grin left them with no doubt as to what was first on the list.

"So what does Adri—?"

Again Eliot cut in. "He doesn't know."

"Oh?"

The disapproving arch in Miriam's eyebrows was even more condemning than that one worded question. Dani reacted by turning her back on the both of them, filling her watering can and going to tend the plants lined up like refugees on her windowsill.

One thing she'd loved about growing up in Montana, was working with her mother in their large vegetable and flower gardens. She didn't have a yard in her condo, obviously. But she collected houseplants from people who didn't have green thumbs. Her collection included an English Ivy from Eliot, a Jade plant from Miriam and several African violets from Mr. Boswell down the hall. Usually by the time people gave her their plants, they were almost dead. But she watered, fertilized and pinched them back to health, like a fussy mother hen.

Gently, Dani touched one of the velvety leaves of the plant she'd just finished dousing with water. Two years ago, this delicate violet had been flowerless, with only a half dozen green leaves still on the stem. Now it displayed a profusion of pink flowers. She found this very satisfying. And calming.

"Okay. Enough avoiding the subject," Miriam said firmly. "Have you really not told Adrian that you're pregnant with his baby?"

Dani folded her arms defensively over her chest. "I'm telling him on Sunday. We have lunch plans."

"You mean he actually slotted you in on the weekend?" Miriam gave her a thumbs up.

"Only because Ava's been invited to a neighbor's birthday party." It was ridiculous, but sometimes her relationship with Adrian felt almost illicit. They were two unmarried, consenting adults. It shouldn't be this difficult.

"Are you afraid he's going to ask you to terminate?" Miriam asked.

Dani stared at her, astounded. Miriam was always blunt. But this was a bit much—or was it? Maybe the reason she objected to the question was because she was afraid it might be true. "I have no idea how he's going to react," she admitted. "I'm hoping—he'll feel the same as me."

Miriam and Eliot exchanged a quick glance. The flash of doubt in their faces told Dani that they were worried she was going to get hurt. But they didn't know Adrian. And they'd always been prejudiced against him.

"Well, whatever Adrian says, this *is* exciting news." Miriam crossed the room and offered her arms. Dani had to crouch a little to hug the petite woman, but it did feel nice all the same.

"If you need someone to take you maternity clothes shopping, I'm your girl."

Dani smiled her gratitude. "That's exactly what I need."

"But first a Rumi Cube tournament," Eliot said, slipping his phone back into his pocket. "And some real cocktails.

Give me a minute to hunt down the ingredients for virgin mojitos. I have some fresh mint in my fridge."

"Virgin? You guys don't have to stop drinking alcohol because of me."

"Consider it an act of solidarity." Eliot flashed her a smile before taking off on his mission. As he closed the door, Miriam let out a groan.

"When did you say your baby is due?"

"September eighth."

"That's a long time to go without alcohol."

Dani put a hand on her stomach. "Tell me about it."

&ed; &ed;

HAPPY HOUR PARTIES usually lasted well past midnight, but by ten o'clock that evening, Dani had her home to herself. Eliot had taken his iPod with him so the place was quiet. Her blender was soaking in the sink. She wasn't sure if the green scum would ever come off. Eliot's concoction of virgin mojitos had actually tasted great—and had even looked pretty when served in her fancy margarita glasses.

But the lack of alcohol had definitely put a damper on the evening. Miriam, in her usual forthright way, had said it best.

"I'm not sure I like you guys when you're sober."

Was that the problem? Were they all dull when they weren't drinking?

It was a sobering—ha-ha—thought.

But not, Dani suspected, the truth.

It was her news that had taken the fizz out of the evening. Eliot and Miriam weren't sure how to treat her now. And they were apprehensive about her decision to keep the baby, Dani could tell.

Which made her just the smallest bit angry. Just because they couldn't imagine raising a child, didn't mean they should automatically assume she was incapable.

Only—maybe she was? Especially if the baby was born with extra challenges.

All night she'd been avoiding thinking about what the ultrasound had shown. But the worry had planted like a seed in her gut and it was growing larger with every hour. She'd studied Down Syndrome in a Life Span Development course when she was getting her masters. She understood the science, knew that the congenital defects were the result of an extra twenty-first chromosome.

In practical terms, a baby with Down Syndrome was going to have both cognitive and physical challenges, of varying degrees of severity.

Dani went into the room she used for her office, custom designed with built-in bookshelves and drawers she used for her files. The long desk faced an oil painting of Paradise Valley, her long-ago Montana home. There were no ranches or buildings of any kind in her painting. Just nature. Mountains and sky that took on different hues depending on the amount of light coming in the window. That was true in real life, too. Depending on the time of day, and even her mood, she always saw something different when she was driving the long road that curved along the floor of that valley. The painting reminded her that while she hadn't enjoyed growing up on a ranch, she'd been lucky to be surrounded by so much beauty.

She sat in her office chair, then swiveled to face the filing cabinets. It took only a few minutes to locate her old notes from the Life Span course. She had a very organized filing system.

Once she'd scanned through that information, she still had questions, so she turned to the Internet. She searched for books and downloaded a few. She devoured several of the stories about children and their families and found them reassuring. Many of the less-severely affected children eventually reached the same milestones as "normal" children. They sat up and crawled, learned to walk, and eventually to talk as well. Some were able to graduate high school, hold a job, and in many respects live a so-called "normal" life.

It's going to be okay. If it happens—I can handle it.

But. There was a good chance it *wouldn't* happen. Her research had reassured her that Down Syndrome couldn't be identified accurately via ultrasound at sixteen weeks. She wasn't going to panic. After all, she was under the age threshold of thirty-five years, at which point the chances of a mother having an affected baby went up.

Yeah. But only one year under that threshold…

Eventually, she went to bed. And eventually she also fell asleep.

❧ ❦

DAMN IT, THIS was stupid. Eliot rolled over in bed frustrated that he was still awake. He *never* had trouble sleeping. But he couldn't stop thinking about Dani and the fact that she was pregnant. How could she have let that happen? Bad enough that she was dating—or sneaking around with—that self-absorbed bastard from her work. Eliot had been waiting for her to come to her senses and realize she deserved more from a man than occasional dinners and romps in the sack.

But this was a big setback to that plan.

Finally, he fell asleep, but only fitfully. When dawn came he was happy to give up on a lost cause and go out for his morning run. Often Dani joined him, but today it was too early to knock on her door and ask her along.

Just as well. Eliot needed some thinking time. He set a pace faster than usual, but not fast enough to escape the basic facts of the situation. Dani Carrigan, the woman who was supposed to soon realize that Adrian Carlson was a jerk and break up with him, now seemed to be in more in love with the cad than ever. And was having his baby.

That last one was the zinger. Eliot had stick-handled enough divorces to know that it wasn't marriage certificates that kept couples together. It was children. This baby would forever tie Dani and Adrian together, which he was sure was not in Dani's best interests.

Not that Eliot was in love with Dani himself. But he did like her and consider her one of the loveliest women he'd ever met. She was brainy, but sweet, and despite her sophistication in many areas had remnants of country charm that he found completely disarming.

A woman of Dani Carrigan's caliber deserved a man who placed her at the center of his world. Not in a corner.

After his five mile route, Eliot showered and tried to read the morning paper until he judged it was late enough to call on Dani. He went out first, to pick up flowers and a take-out breakfast sandwich from B.B.'s. He bought one for himself, too, and downed the delicious egg, cheese and spinach sandwiched between halves of a warm buttermilk biscuit, in four bites.

Yum. Apparently his sleepless night wasn't affecting his appetite.

It was just after ten when he tapped on Dani's door. As soon as he saw her he could tell she'd had a restless night, too.

"Trouble sleeping?"

"Yeah. I mostly read and watched old episodes of *The Big Bang Theory.*"

He didn't admit to his own insomnia, because the under-lying causes had to be concealed. If he confessed her predicament had rendered him sleepless, too, she might jump to some wrong conclusions about his feelings for her. For instance, the urge he had to pull her into his arms right now was merely friendly. But since that, too, might be misconstrued he merely kissed her lightly on the forehead before presenting her with the spring blossoms.

"For the mother-to-be. Miriam and I were in shock yesterday. Forgive us if we weren't appropriately congratula-tory."

"Thank you. They're beautiful." She added water, then placed them on the low table in the living room. As she padded back to the kitchen table, she focused on his soft leather loafers, then glanced up past the pressed blue jeans to his striped shirt and linen blazer, both rolled up at the cuffs.

She shook her head. "You look so good. And you've already showered, which means you've been out for your run. And been shopping. What time did you get up?"

"Six.-Ish."

"I used to have energy once, too. I think. Back in the days when I could still drink caffeine."

"You do look tired. And aren't those the same clothes you were wearing yesterday?" He hadn't thought Lycra could wrinkle. But hers certainly had. That didn't stop her from looking beautiful. Dani was always beautiful. And so gorgeously unaware of the fact.

"I don't have anything else that fits."

"Not even pajamas?"

"You can tell I slept in this?"

"Um. Yeah." His gaze swept over her uncombed hair and make-up free face. "Tell me you've had breakfast, at least."

"Milk and my multi-vitamin."

"Mom cannot live on milk alone," he announced, handing her the B.B. bag.

"Oh my gosh. Amazing. How did you know I was craving one of these?" She bit hungrily into the sandwich, then mumbled her thanks.

He pulled out his phone and called Miriam. "I'm at Dani's and I'm staging an intervention. You have to take her shopping. Now. Okay, I'll give you half an hour. No longer." When he'd ended the call, he added, "I suggest you do something with your hair before Miriam gets here."

Dani set the sandwich aside for a moment, so she could grab her brush and an elastic from the bathroom. "I'd forgotten what it's like to have a mom. You're good at it."

He perched on one of the kitchen stools and regarded her thoughtfully. He'd lost his mother when he was nineteen. Dani, when she was sixteen. They talked about it sometimes, the way it hurt. The way the missing never stopped, not even now that they were adults.

But it had been so much harder for her than him. She'd only been sixteen and her father had been useless. She'd had to step into the role of mother to her younger sisters. Which was why, she'd once told him, she didn't think she'd ever have kids.

Obviously, she'd changed her mind on that score.

"I feel like I hardly slept at all last night, but I must have dropped off for a few hours at least, because I dreamt about my Mom."

Dani had managed to pull her hair into a presentable ponytail. The style showcased the perfect bone structure of her face, the sweet curve of her lips and the blue of her eyes. She'd set down the brush and was now staring out the window, in the dreamy way of someone who wasn't really living in the present.

"Was it a good dream?"

"Yeah. She came into my room and kissed my forehead. She told me not to stay up too late reading."

"I bet your Mom used to say that to you a lot."

"All the time. But she would never turn the light out. Because she understood. Mom and I were alike in that way.

26

She loved to read too."

Dani had told him this before. But he still listened. Just the way she listened to him when he felt like talking about his mother. He wondered if any of Dani's sisters realized what a misfit she'd felt like growing up with them all on the Circle C Ranch. Sage, Callan and Mattie were all accomplished riders, athletic and great lovers of the outdoors. Whereas Dani—and her mother—felt more at home in the world of books.

"How do you think your mom would have felt about—" he glanced at her waistline—"the baby?"

"Happy, I think. That's one of the hardest things. Not being able to tell her. Not *ever* being able to share the experience of motherhood with her."

As a man Eliot doubted he could fully comprehend what the loss meant to Dani. But he could sure see how sad she felt.

"My very last memory of Mom is seeing her standing in my bedroom doorway, looking back at me with a smile before closing the door. I wish I'd known then that in less than two hours—"

She didn't finish her sentence, because she didn't need to. Eliot knew her mother had been killed in the barn late that night, while she and her husband were trying to help a heifer with a difficult delivery. Distressed and in great pain, the heifer had lashed out at Dani's mother, causing instant death.

Dani turned from the window, focusing her amazing, faded-blue jean colored eyes on him. "What's your last memory of your Mom?"

He cleared his throat. "She came into my room to ask if I thought her scarf went with her new coat." His mom hadn't had daughters to ask such questions of, and so she'd turned to him, her youngest son. Frankly, he'd been happy to oblige. He'd always had a good eye for color.

"And did it?"

"No. But I told her it did, because I knew they were running late. Dad was already out in the car, revving the engine the way he always did when Mom kept him waiting."

If only he'd told his mother the truth. Then his mom would have gone to her room to select a different scarf and his parents would have departed for their party a few minutes later. They wouldn't have been in the intersection when the teenage driver paying more attention to text messages than the road, ran the red light.

&

WHEN IT CAME to shopping, Miriam knew what she was doing. She navigated while Dani drove, taking them first to Sugarlump where Dani purchased gray slacks, a plum-colored skirt and two dresses for work. Currently her tops and blazers still fit and she thought they still would for at least a month. She also bought underwear. "Bras. I need bigger bras."

Her breasts, actually, were what had first tipped her off she was pregnant. They'd tingled and become super-sensitive. Now her pretty B cups had expanded into C.

She allowed Miriam into the change room to see. "If this

keeps up I'll be into triple G by the time I give birth."

Miriam winced. "Wonder what will happen when you shrink back to normal?"

"Yeah." Dani stared at her image in the mirror. Was this the end? Was she now on a downward slope that would whisk her into middle-aged frumpiness?

"On the bright side, you look pretty hot right now. Buy the bra. It's perfect."

On the way out of the store, another purchase added to her canvas shopping bag, Dani reminded herself that her sister Mattie, five years older than her, had delivered twins, and still looked great. Yes, Dani's body was about to be invaded, stretched and re-shaped. But it would snap back. Eventually.

But would her life be equally elastic?

What were her days going to be like once she had a baby? How would she juggle work, time with friends, her running and social life?

Truth was, she couldn't imagine any of it. She was holding on to a slim hope that somehow Adrian was going to provide the solution to all her problems. Her stomach tightened—Nerves? Excitement?—as she anticipated their lunch tomorrow. Less than twenty-four hours now.

"Hungry?" Miriam asked.

"Starved," she admitted. Even though she'd eaten every crumb of the breakfast sandwich Eliot had bought for her.

"Well, you can't eat until you've bought some jeans. I checked online and Village Maternity carries Citizens of Humanity. We'll go there next. I don't ever want to see you in those yoga pants again."

Dani smiled. "What if I'm doing yoga?"

"Well. *Maybe* then. But just maybe."

❧ ❧

THE NEXT DAY Dani was grateful to Miriam for taking her shopping. She wore her new maternity jeans with a pink linen blouse and wedge sandals. Her hair was long, in soft curls, and she'd put on her usual make-up trio—eye liner, mascara and lip gloss. She turned this way and that in front of her mirror. You had to look closely to see the baby bump.

But it was there.

She took a cab to the restaurant, purposefully arriving ten minutes late because she wanted this meeting to be different. Usually, she was the on-time one, with no six-year-old daughter to serve as an excuse. But today, she wanted Adrian to have his eyes on her as she walked toward his table. She pictured him smiling, rising from his chair and opening his arms. She had it all worked out and so it was disappointing to discover that he still hadn't arrived, wasn't waiting at all.

She was escorted to their reserved table by the window. First thing, she checked her phone, but there was no message warning her he was running late.

"Would you like something to drink, Miss?" The waiter, a young male whose appreciative gaze told her that she was, indeed, looking good, set down two menus.

"Water is fine for now." She thought back to when she'd first met Adrian, at a meeting shortly after he'd accepted the posting for faculty head. He'd looked Italian to her, with his thick dark hair and olive skin.

And his eyes—they were soulful and sad, wise and perceptive. She'd felt as if they'd established a special connection from the moment he looked at her and said her name.

"Dr. Carrigan. Yes. I'm familiar with your work. As a father, I find it very interesting."

Her work—the reason she was here in Seattle at the University of Washington—was with the much respected Dr. Jenna Dayton. Jenna was interested in the infant's sensitivity to fairness and early pro-social behavior and how that linked to later academic success. They'd just completed a major research paper and released a jointly written article that had been getting a lot of attention.

Dani had felt gratified by Adrian Carlson's acknowledgment. And she wasn't put off by the mention of a daughter, either. Like everyone else, she knew Dr. Carlson's circumstances, that his wife had died tragically, that he'd re-located with his daughter needing to make a new start.

Dani wasn't used to looking to colleagues—especially those in positions higher than hers—for dating prospects.

But Adrian was the kind of man a woman was lucky to meet once in her lifetime. He had the polite manners of a European, combined with a brilliant intellect and a sharp wit. How could she resist?

If he hadn't been attracted to her, too, she would have been spared.

But she could tell, from the start, that he was.

The way his eyes would dart to hers when something was

said that struck him as interesting or clever. The way he rolled his pen with his long elegant fingers when they were alone, later, at the end of the meeting. She looked at those fingers and imagined them on her skin—

"Darling. I'm sorry I've kept you waiting."

She'd been daydreaming so hadn't noticed him enter the restaurant. Now, Adrian was at the table, bending to kiss her before taking a seat.

"Ava was so excited about going to this party. Then when it was time for me to actually leave, she turned clingy. I was afraid I was going to have cancel our lunch entirely, but fortunately, the mother hosting the party brought out supplies for a craft—making a sock puppet or something— and instantly I was extraneous. Ava wouldn't even hug me goodbye."

Dani heard the words, but didn't take in their meaning. She was focused on the way he called her *darling*, his favorite endearment for her. Adrian never dropped the "g" the way flirtatious cowboys back in Montana often did. His darling sounded smooth and sophisticated.

She sipped her water, trying to push away the resentment she felt about his late arrival. This was supposed to be a happy occasion. She couldn't begin by nursing a grudge.

The waiter returned and before she could intervene, Adrian had ordered them a bottle of a Sonoma Syrah. "I've been looking forward to seeing you all weekend," he said, reaching for one of her hands. "I'm glad you wore that blouse. You look so feminine in pink."

He stroked the skin on her hand gently, slowly, suggestively.

"It's been a long time since we made love."

"Yes." She studied his eyes. Was this her opening? But before she could get out the right words, Adrian was talking again.

"There's a boutique hotel down the street. What do you say we rent a room after lunch?"

They'd never done that before. It sounded extravagant to Dani. But also erotic.

"Maybe. But there is something—"

The waiter was back with the wine and two glasses. Dani let him pour some of the Syrah into her glass, not wanting to make a big deal about not drinking until she'd delivered her news.

When they were alone again, she leaned in close and lowered her voice. "If you're wondering if I've been avoiding having sex with you the past while—the answer is yes."

Adrian looked shocked. Hurt. "Darling. You're not happy with me?"

"No, no, that's not what I'm trying to say. I didn't want you to see me naked."

"But—why? Your body is beautiful, Danielle. You know how much I love it. How much I *need* it."

Why was it so hard to tell him? Maybe she should have done it over the phone. Not to mention sooner.

"I'm pregnant, Adrian."

She watched his face go completely still. It was like the switch to his personality had been powered off. She understood. He was pulling into himself. Processing her words.

Slowly he withdrew his hand, bringing it up as if to ward off a blow.

"But—" He fell silent again. "The night of the Christmas party. When we found that back room—?"

"Yes." She'd worn a strapless red dress to their faculty Christmas dinner. The dinner had been organized in a restaurant that catered to small business gatherings. Their party had run late, and she and Adrian were the last to go. He'd been expected home—his nanny wanted to spend the night at her sister's, because they were catching a plane together early the next morning. So he'd found a little room, pulled her inside and closed the door.

"You've been driving me crazy all night long. Where did you get this dress? Oh, my God, you look so beautiful."

She remembered the heat of his mouth on her neck, shoulders, back. She'd gone to the bathroom earlier, removed her panties. When his hands travelled up her legs and found her nakedness, he'd groaned in her ear.

"You are so wicked, Danielle. And I love it."

He'd hitched up her dress, unzipped his pants and taken her there, with her back pressed against the wooden door.

The one and only time they'd taken no precautions.

She'd expected him to pull out in time, but he hadn't. "I'm sorry," he'd whispered. "That just felt too good."

Well, how was it feeling now? she wondered. He still hadn't said a word to her.

"That was—four months ago," he finally said.

"Yes. I'm sixteen weeks along."

He brushed a hand through his hair, a familiar gesture

when he was confused. "You haven't said a word."

"I was—" She ran her finger around the rim of her wineglass. "I think I was sort of in denial."

"Being pregnant isn't the sort of problem that gets smaller with time, Danielle."

Problem. "I know."

"Have you—do you know how you want to deal with this?"

He looked anxious. A fine sheen of moisture had popped out on his brow and upper lip.

He began fiddling with the white linen napkin, folding it first one way, then the other. His gaze had dropped to the table, too. No matter how hard she stared at him, willing him to raise his head, she couldn't get him to look at her.

"Obviously, an abortion would erase the entire *problem* for you," she said.

For just a second, his eyes flashed up and she saw the hope in them.

"But it's not that easy for me," she added.

"Danielle, you're an academic. One of the brightest people I know. So far you've made very smart decisions in your life. You're only thirty-five and already you've earned a reputation with your research. In five years, you'll be eligible for tenure."

Actually, she was thirty-four, she wanted to say. But she was too focused on the way he'd said, *your* life. Not *our* life.

"Having a baby wouldn't stop me from going back to work, continuing my research. It wouldn't disqualify me for tenure."

"No." He was quiet for a while, waving away the waiter when he tried to approach for a food order, sipping down half a glass of wine. His gaze went to the untouched glass on her side of the table. "Are we having a discussion here? Or have you already made up your mind?"

She felt as if he was underscoring a line he'd already drawn between them with words like "problem" and "your life." And it hurt. She'd finally come to him with this, hoping to share some of the burden. But he was handing it right back to her.

"As you're the father, of course I care what you think."

"To a point," he said with some bitterness.

"Is there no part of you that sees this as good news?"

"God, you make me feel like a monster for saying no. But the last two years have been hard. Dealing with Vanessa's death. Trying to be a good father to Ava. Let me tell you from experience, being a single parent isn't easy."

Did it not even occur to him that there was another answer here? That the two of them could make a life together? Raise his Ava and their baby as one family?

"I guess I should have asked this sooner. But what have the past six months meant to you? What do *I* mean to you?" From under the table, Dani clenched her hands, preparing herself for some hard-hitting truths, and the fact that Eliot and Miriam may have been right about this relationship all along.

"Danielle, I adore you. I truly do. I think about all the time. I *want* you all the time. But after six months, I'm not ready to say we should get married. And I'm not going to let an unplanned pregnancy rush me into making such a serious decision. Especially not when I should be putting Ava's best interests ahead of everything."

This time it was Dani who bowed her head, Dani who couldn't lift her gaze to meet his.

Everything he said was perfectly sensible. She understood instinctively that he wasn't trying to hurt her. He was being careful and protecting his daughter.

"So—if I decide to keep the baby—do you want to stop seeing one another?"

He sighed. "I'm not going to desert you. Or walk away from my share of responsibility."

Was he talking money now? She hesitated to ask, in case he started to think that was what she'd been after all along. When it totally wasn't. Sure, they'd only been seeing each other for half a year. But it was long enough for her to know she loved him. Where would he find anyone more perfectly suited to him, than her? They shared common interests, enjoyed spending time together and had great chemistry.

So what was missing?

Why wasn't six months long enough for him to love her, too?

❧ ❧

DANI AND ADRIAN eventually ordered food, which they ate with little enjoyment. Adrian didn't finish the bottle of red. But he came close. He didn't mention the boutique hotel again, and Dani didn't dare remind him of the idea. Her news had been a real mood-buster. She got that.

She saw now how totally naïve she'd been to hope that on some level Adrian might see the baby as good news.

He'd made it pretty clear that he'd prefer the problem to just—disappear. And he'd be even more determined for her to have an abortion if he knew there was a chance the child had Downs.

So easy for him to say. But to him the abortion was an abstract procedure. He wouldn't have to book time off work, submit his body for the surgery—and feel the loss of the life that was currently inside her.

Tears dripped down to her eggs Florentine. Adrian didn't notice. He was on his phone, scrolling through emails or something.

She could imagine how Miriam and Eliot would react if they were here, witnessing this scene. They'd be so angry on her behalf. And they'd wonder why she wasn't angry, too.

But how could she be, when it was easy to see Adrian's side? He was right when he said keeping the baby didn't make sense for her from a career or financial viewpoint. Normally she was a logical person. So she understood where he was coming from.

Yet, every instinct in her body was urging her to protect and nurture the little life within. At age thirty-four this wasn't necessarily her last chance to have a baby. However fertility rates in women dropped sharply after thirty-five, so it might be.

After Adrian paid the bill, he accompanied her outside, where a gentle drizzle had them lingering under the awning to say their goodbyes. Adrian took her hands. "We need to talk about this some more. But first I want you to think. Life is good for you—for us—right now. All of that will change if you decide to keep this baby."

This baby. Not *our* baby.

"Fair enough. But I'd like you to try and see this from my point of view. It's easy to tell someone to have an abortion. But actually *doing* it…?"

"That would be hard. I understand. But sometimes doing the right thing *is* hard." He swallowed, then squeezed her hands. "*Very* hard."

Dani thought of the barn cats at the Circle C, how sometimes they'd given birth to unexpected litters and her father had taken the unwanted kittens down to Serendipity Creek. How she and her sisters had cried. Her mother, too, turning her back so she wouldn't see.

But Dani had.

It was one thing to say you believed in a woman's right to choose. She did believe that. As had her mother, and the minister at their church. But when the choice was yours to make, then it got personal.

"Let's have dinner on Wednesday," Adrian said. "Your place. I'll order Thai food, if that's okay."

She nodded. If the conversation had gone differently, she would have told him that she had a doctor's appointment on Wednesday afternoon and invited him to come with her.

As it was, she didn't.

❧ ❦

DANI WAS SO nervous the day of her doctor's appointment,

she could hardly eat. She'd been lucky enough to have only brief periods of nausea so far in her pregnancy, so she didn't blame hormones. This was all nerves.

She had a class to teach in the morning, her Intro to Psych class. It was held in an auditorium-style lecture hall holding hundreds of students, one of whom was her niece, Portia. Mattie's daughters were both beautiful and petite like their mother. While Wren was the more studious of the two, and in this way so much more similar to Dani, for some reason she had always had a closer connection to Portia who was sweet and loved fashion and boys more than she seemed to care for books.

Dani knew that while her sister had encouraged her daughters to move away from their home at Bishop Stables near Big Arm, Montana, to go to college, she'd hoped that they would both pick the University of Washington where they would have each other—and their Aunt Dani—for moral support.

But Wren had chosen to go her own way, moving to Boulder where she attended the University of Colorado. Besides being academically inclined, Wren was also the more self-sufficient of the twins, something Dani didn't think Mattie had appreciated until after the twins had left home.

And maybe that was why Dani felt a stronger connection to Portia. Portia *needed* people and she liked being around family. She also sort of hero-worshipped Dani, always commenting on how much she liked the clothes her aunt wore, the Volvo coup she drove, her elegant condo. Portia went so far as to copy the way Dani styled her hair and applied her make-up.

The first time Portia had been in her luxury condo she'd exclaimed, "I feel like I'm in a movie!"

Before Christmas, when Portia's parents had first decided to split up, Portia had gone through a rough patch. She'd spent too much time partying and hanging out with the wrong friends. Her grades had suffered, too. But over the holidays, she'd had good visits with both of her parents, and had come back to college a more mature young woman.

Dani had been relieved when she stopped hanging out with the party animals and began focusing more on her studies.

She also seemed to have a new guy in her life, and often sat beside him in class. A tall, skinny, dark-haired boy named Austin Bradshaw. The kid's hair was always in his eyes but he had a disarmingly nice smile. Dani could only name a handful of her students, but she knew Austin. He had the best grades in the class.

He was also, she understood from Portia, a novice rodeo competitor. This summer he planned to earn money on the circuit, riding bulls and bareback broncos. Dani had been meaning to invite the two of them for dinner one night. But the pregnancy had derailed her in more ways than one. She really needed to be a better aunt.

After class, Dani waved at her niece, indicating that she wanted to talk. This was a lot easier to do now that Portia no longer chose to sit in the far back rows. Portia said a few words to Austin, who nodded then took off. Portia waited until the stream of students leaving the hall had ebbed before making her way down to the lectern where Dani was slipping her notes back into her briefcase.

Dani gave her niece a hug. "I'm sorry I didn't call you this Sunday. It's been a while since we've had one of our dinners."

"That's okay. I went over to Austin's. He lives with his dad and they're both really good cooks."

"You and Austin seem to be getting along well."

Portia's cheeks turned pink. "Yeah. Though sometimes I wonder if he likes my dad more than me. He knows more about Dad's years in the rodeo than I do."

Wes Bishop had been a rodeo cowboy when Mattie met him, and he'd remained one throughout their almost twenty years of marriage. There was no doubt all the travel and time apart had put a strain on their marriage and had led to its ultimate break-down.

But Dani felt that the two of them were at their core incompatible, both wanting something different out of life. It seemed like they were in the process now of working that out. She hoped they would both end up happier—and not hurt Portia or Wren too much in the process.

"Have you talked to your sister and mom lately?"

"Wren is good. With Mom it's hard to tell. She and dad, well…you know."

Dani felt a twinge of guilt. Sage had gone to visit Mattie when her marital problems first started. She should try to take a trip out to Montana, as well. But given what was going on in her life, she just couldn't see how to make it work. Perhaps the best she could at this time was make sure

Portia was doing okay.

"Would you and Austin like come over to my place for dinner this coming Sunday?"

"Thanks, I'd love that. Not sure about Austin. He has a big paper due on Monday."

"Well, if he finishes early, let me know. I'd be happy to see him, too. Sunday around six o'clock?"

"Thanks!" Portia gave her a farewell hug and Dani wondered if she'd noticed her aunt's thickening waistline. She—and the rest of the family—would soon have to be told soon.

But first, Dani had to put in a few hours at the lab. Then go to her doctor's appointment.

Normally, Dani loved the hours she spent with Dr. Jenna Dayton at the Early Childhood Cognition Lab. She and Jenna had met at a conference three years ago. Jenna was about eight years older, a freckled, golden-haired woman with an incredible ability to focus intently on whatever subject was at hand.

She and Jenna had several long conversations at the conference, and about a week later Jenna had expressed interest in having Dani move to Seattle and join her research team. It had taken a while to organize the new job, but eventually it all came together. Dani was thrilled at the chance to live again in the city she'd enjoyed so much in her undergrad years. More importantly Jenna's offer gave her the chance to focus on research she found fascinating: studying fairness and how the concept developed in preschool children and then played out in academic success later in life.

Dani and Jenna were looking for answers to questions

like: At what age did a child develop a concept of fairness? Was a sense of fair play innate to humans? Or did children have to be socialized to perceive it? And did the ability to perceive and care about fairness have any impact on later academic success?

Their biggest challenge at this early stage of research was designing tests for children who were too young to communicate by means of language.

But this challenge was also what made the work so interesting.

The hours after lunch flew by for Dani, and she might have missed her doctor's appointment if she hadn't set her phone to give her a thirty minute reminder. She closed down her laptop and put away her papers. "I have an appointment," she told Jenna, working across the hall in her neat-as-a-pin office.

Jenna gave a distracted nod. "See you tomorrow," she mumbled.

Outside the day was moody, hinting at rain but not quite delivering it. Dani hurried to the clinic where she'd had her ultrasound last Friday and where her obstetrician, Gwen Fong, had her office.

This would be her third appointment with the doctor, and compared to this one the first two had been a breeze. She'd been lucky to have a relatively easy first trimester, with only fatigue and occasional nausea to deal with. From her conversations in the waiting room, she knew other women were not so fortunate.

But it seemed fate had caught up to her at last.

What would Dr. Fong have to say about that ultrasound? Now that she was about to find out, Dani wondered if she had the courage to deal with what lay ahead.

The first part of her appointment went fine. She was measured and weighed. Her blood pressure looked good, all was progressing as normal. Then Dr. Fong came into the room and took a seat in the chair next to the examining table upon which Dani was sitting.

Dr. Fong was barely five feet tall, with an apple-shaped body, round face, tiny pointed chin, and kind brown eyes. Those eyes met Dani's directly as she lowered her voice and said, "About your ultrasound…"

Dani realized she was holding her breath. She let out the air wishing she had a hand to cling to other than her own.

She missed the first couple of sentences the doctor said. "Pardon me?"

Patiently the doctor went over the facts again. "Your screen test results suggest you're at risk of having a baby with Down Syndrome. What happens next is up to you."

"M-my choices?"

"You can choose to undergo diagnostic testing, to find out for sure. There are three options here." The doctor opened a file and pulled out a brochure. "Here. You might want to follow along with this while I explain."

She pointed to a heading *Amniocentesis*.

"This is a procedure that tests the amniotic fluid surrounding the fetus."

Dani had read about this in her pregnancy books. Another purpose of the amniocentesis was to predict the sex of the baby. She wished that was her primary concern right now. But the test, as she recalled, carried risks. "What's the chance that an amniocentesis could result in miscarriage?"

"It isn't trivial," Dr. Wong admitted. "About one in every two hundred."

"So if I take the test, I could lose a perfectly healthy baby?"

"That is possible, unfortunately." Dr. Fong flipped the page of the brochure and pointed to a new heading. "However the other two screening tests carry even higher risks. Chorionic villus sampling—where we take cells from your placenta to analyze the fetal chromosomes—has about a doubled risk of miscarriage compared to the amniocentesis. While percutaneous umbilical blood sampling—where blood from a vein in the umbilical cord is examined for chromosomal defects—is even riskier. I wouldn't recommend we do that unless the test from the amniocentesis was unclear."

The information washed over Dani like words spoken in a foreign language. She stared at the headings in the brochure and tried to focus. "How much time do I have to decide?"

"The sooner the better. In case you decide not to carry the baby to term."

The word "abortion," though unspoken, hung in the air between them. Dani wished she had someone who loved her sitting in that empty chair, someone to help her weigh the pros and the cons.

"What would you do if you were in my position?"

Dr. Fong leaned back on her stool. "I don't have to

speculate. I was in your situation, three years ago when I was pregnant with my second child."

Suddenly the barrier between doctor and patient slipped away and in that instant Dani felt they were two women talking heart to heart. "So you had an abnormal ultrasound, too?"

Dr. Fong nodded.

"And you—?"

"Opted to have an amniocentesis. In our case the results were negative. We had a perfectly healthy little boy. I wish I could guarantee you the same outcome. But I can't."

"No. I understand." She hesitated. "What would you have done if the result was positive for Downs?"

"I can't tell you. My husband thought we should terminate for the sake of our first child. But I—I really can't say what we would have decided if we had been faced with that scenario."

Dr. Fong got up from the stool and made some entries on the computer at the corner of the examining room. As she typed, she still managed to speak. "Go home and discuss this with your family. You can call the office with your decision about whether to take the tests. Don't rush your decision, but if you could get back to us within a few days, that would be good."

☙ ❧

"YOUR NEW CLIENT is in reception. I've put a thermos of coffee in the small conference room, as well as pitcher of ice water." Paige Blythe unearthed a small notebook from beneath a mound of papers on Eliot's desk. She was looking very spring-like today in a floral dress accessorized with dangling tangerine-colored earrings. It was the sort of outfit only a woman in her twenties, like Paige, could get away with.

His assistant's temperament matched the cheery colors she was wearing. She was also well organized, efficient and had the special talent of always knowing where Eliot misplaced things. In the three years they'd worked together, she'd managed to become invaluable to him, and he accepted the notebook gratefully. He'd tried attending meetings with just his i-Pad, but found the electronic tablet created a barrier between him and his clients. Real paper and pens were friendlier.

"Thanks, Paige." Quickly he flipped to where he'd jotted down information from his initial phone call with this client. Lizbeth Greenway, married in the state of Washington eight years to Nick Greenway. No children. Currently separated from spouse and looking to initiate divorce proceedings. Both spouses worked at Allez—an on-line service designed to be a one-stop destination for working parents, offering everything from diaper services to "build a playground in your backyard" kits. The firm had recently gone public and based on market cap was currently worth about twenty million.

Successful, jointly-owned companies tended to make for messy divorces, Eliot reflected as he made his way to the reception area. But as soon as he saw Lizbeth Greenway get up from the chocolate brown leather chair to shake his hand, he realized the case was going to be even more complicated than he'd thought.

Lizbeth Greenway was pregnant.

Her baby bump was small, but clearly outlined by the stretchy tunic top she was wearing over skinny jeans and fashionable heels.

This reminded him of Dani, and for a second he lost his composure. He hadn't spoken to her since her lunch date with Adrian on Sunday. He knew that secretly she'd hoped Adrian would be thrilled about the baby. Thrilled enough to ask her to marry him.

But if that had happened, Eliot figured Dani would have called him and Miriam to share the good news.

So it probably hadn't happened that way. And Eliot felt guilty about being happy that it hadn't.

"Eliot Gilmore?"

Quickly he recharged his smile and held out a hand. "Nice to meet you, Lizbeth." They'd already agreed to skip formalities in their initial phone conversation. "My assistant Paige has set things up for us in one of the small meeting rooms." He gestured to the open door that led out of reception, then waited for her to precede him. "Turn left, and it's the first door on your right."

He followed her into the conference room, almost shutting the door, but leaving a one inch gap. Being alone with female clients in closed rooms was something he avoided.

Especially beautiful, young ones. Even if they were pregnant.

He placed Lizbeth in her mid-thirties. She had wavy

auburn hair, a wide mouth that probably looked lovely when she smiled and deeply set brown eyes, which were currently shimmering with moisture.

These tears were as yet unshed. But by her blotchy skin and puffy eyes he could tell she'd done a lot of crying lately.

"Beautiful sunny morning, isn't it?" The window was south-facing and the room was bright as a result. The light caught the colors of the oil painting on the far wall, bringing out the shades of blue, gray and white in the ocean scene. On the small, circular table was the promised thermos of coffee, a tray with sugar and cream, coffee mugs and spoons, as well as the pitcher of water and tall crystal glasses. Tucked in amid all this was a box of tissues.

Initial consults could get very emotional.

"Thanks for fitting me in to your schedule. My friend's aunt highly recommended you."

He gave her a warm smile. "I'm happy to get referrals. Not so keen on repeat business."

Her eyes widened, and then she smiled. He'd been right. She had a great smile.

It didn't last long, however. Her bottom lip quivered and she lowered her head. "This is so hard. I never thought this could happen to Nick and me."

He offered her coffee, then felt like an idiot when she explained she was avoiding caffeine because it wasn't good for the baby.

He thought of Dani again. How could he have missed noticing she was pregnant? Showed how observant he was.

"Would you prefer herbal tea?"

"Water is fine."

So he poured her some and took a cup of the black brew for himself. He wished Lizbeth Greenway had mentioned she was pregnant during their initial conversation. He had a spiel he always gave his clients when there were children involved. He hadn't anticipated needing to do that today.

Lizbeth took a sip of water, then set the glass on the table like a gavel. "As I said on the phone, I want to divorce my husband."

"Right. I take it your husband is in agreement with this decision?"

"Sort of."

He raised his eyebrows. "Does he have a lawyer?"

"Not yet." She placed a hand on her belly. "But he will. Nick says the baby isn't his. He's accusing me of cheating on him. What else can we do, but get divorced? He obviously doesn't trust me."

"Once your baby is born, a simple DNA test is all it would take to set his mind at ease. The baby *is* Nick's?"

"Of course it is! And a DNA test wouldn't settle any-thing. It sure wouldn't make me feel like my husband trusted me." She curled her left hand around the glass of water again. The size of the diamond on her ring would have had a greedier attorney salivating.

"Has he trusted you in the past?"

"Yes. Absolutely. You get to know a man when you've been married eight years. You know him even better if you've been business partners the way we have. I've always been sure I could count on Nick in every way. As a partner, a friend and a lover. I'm absolutely shocked that he doesn't feel the same about me."

"Did something happen recently that would explain why he suddenly doubts you?"

"Just the fact that I got pregnant."

"Was it—planned?" Again Eliot had to work not to let thoughts of Dani and her surprise pregnancy distract him.

"We'd been trying to have a baby for years. I was tested and Nick was tested. According to our doctors there was no medical reason it wasn't happening. We thought maybe it was the stress and long hours we put in at work. So I cut back to four-day weeks and took up yoga. And then, amazingly, it happened. And I thought Nick would be so happy. Instead, he went ballistic. I mean, really crazy."

"How long ago was that?"

"About two months ago. We had a big, big fight and he was so angry, I decided to move in with my cousin. I hoped he would calm down and be reasonable. But he hasn't. Just last week he called me at three in the morning, drunk, and demanding the name of the man I'd slept with. I told him that if he really thought I would cheat on him, that maybe we should get divorced. And he—he agreed."

A tear fell from her eye then, and he pushed the box of tissues a little closer toward her. "I know I'm all but a stranger to you, Lizbeth. But can I offer you some advice?"

She dried her eyes, sniffed, then nodded.

"To me if sounds like you and your husband need a good counselor. Not a divorce attorney. At least not yet." He reached into the breast pocket of his blue pin-striped suit, pulling out a business card for a woman therapist he thought highly of. He set it on the table next to her glass of water.

Lizbeth picked up the card, and frowned. "Nick won't go to counselling. I've already asked him."

"Did he say why not?" The absolute refusal to go to counselling was not a good sign and Eliot's hopes for helping this couple save their marriage sank a little. It was possible the husband had been looking for a way out for a while and was using the pregnancy to drive a wedge between them.

"According to Nick, there's no sense in going to counselling if I'm not going to be honest. The man is impossible."

Maybe he was. But, Eliot still felt compelled to give his spiel. "I've been in this business for many years. Long enough to know divorce causes a lot of pain and often costs a ton of money. Those are reasons enough to do your best to avoid one. But when children are involved the stakes get a lot higher. That baby of yours is going to spend its life dealing with the consequences of how you and Nick handle this setback."

"You're preaching to the choir, Eliot. I don't want a divorce. But Nick is making our marriage impossible. I am going to have a baby in four months. I need support right now. Not night after night filled with arguments and distrust."

Eliot tapped the business card again. "I agree. And right now, I say counselling is your best bet."

"Nick will never go for that—" Her eyes brightened as she focused on him. "But I'm sure he'd come to a meeting with you."

Eliot stifled a groan. He was an attorney, not a counsellor. But how could he say no? As he'd pointed out to Lizbeth, a child's future was at stake.

જ ⟡

WHEN SHE GOT home from her doctor's appointment, Dani found a note under her door. "Want to go for a run?"

It was from Eliot of course. Not only did she recognize his scrawled printing, but he had a habit of leaving notes for her, no matter how often she reminded him that he could simply send her a text message.

She'd been planning to flop on the couch and do some binge TV watching.

But the run would be better for her. She typed a simple "yes" and hit "send," before she could change her mind. Then, she went to her room to change into a roomy t-shirt and yoga pants. She was by the front door, tying up her running shoes, when Eliot knocked.

"It's not locked."

He came inside, wearing proper running clothes in coordinating colors, and somehow managing not to look gay. Eliot had a runner's body, tall, lean and totally ripped. Not only did he run every other day, but he also hit the gym three times a week, too.

"Your doctor okay with you running?"

He was sweet sometimes, the way he worried about her. "She says I can continue with my regular activities as long as I feel comfortable. I'm probably going to take it down a notch, though, so if you'd rather run on your own, that's fine."

Eliot already had to slow his pace when they ran together, but he shrugged off her suggestion that he go on his own.

"Nah. I'd rather have the company."

Once she'd finished with her shoes and locked her condo, they jogged down the stairs, then out to the street. In the late afternoon sun Seattle was full of the promise of summer—every growing thing was either vibrantly green or covered with blossoms.

"So how was your day?" she asked as they paused, waiting for the GPS on Eliot's watch to kick in.

"The usual. Except for one client who reminded me of you."

"Oh?"

He pressed a button his watch, then nodded. "Let's go. You set the pace and I'll follow." They started out heading east toward Washington Park Arboretum.

"Why did your client remind you of me?"

"Because she was pregnant. Maybe a little further along."

She thought about that a minute. "And she's getting divorced?"

"That's what she told me."

"Poor woman." She knew him well enough to guess he wasn't happy about the situation either. "Are you trying to talk her out of it?" Eliot had a ten percent success rate when it came to convincing his clients they shouldn't get divorced. Though most people wouldn't call losing business a success.

"I suggested they try counselling." He checked over his shoulder for oncoming traffic, before leading the way across the street and onto the next block.

"Which they won't do. Because you're going to counsel them."

He made a face at her, but didn't try to deny it. Eliot couldn't help himself. He was a natural conciliator.

"Maybe Adrian and I should book a counseling session with you, too."

"I take you your talk on Sunday didn't go well?"

She grimaced. "Not especially."

"Can't say I'm surprised."

She felt a flash of anger at his reaction, even though, logically, she knew it was justified. "He was just shocked, that's all. The next day he sent me a beautiful bouquet of pink roses."

"Don't you prefer tulips?"

She did, damn it. Sometimes it was annoying how well Eliot knew her. "That's not the point. I think he just needs time to get used to the idea of having a second child."

They were at the park now, running north toward the Bay. They'd gone almost two miles and Dani ought to be hitting her stride. Instead she was out of breath and her legs felt like they would really prefer to be stretched out on the sofa. She slackened her pace a bit more. Poor Eliot was doing little more than jogging in place now.

"Sorry. A little out of shape, I guess."

"Hey, no problem. Why don't we walk for a bit?"

"Thanks. Do you mind if we turn back? That coffee house we just passed looked open."

Usually, they waited until after their run to grab a snack.

But she was feeling light-headed, and some food seemed like a smart idea.

Eliot put a hand on her back. "You sure you're okay? You look pale. Normally your face is as red as a strawberry when we go running."

"I didn't eat much for lunch," she recalled. "I had a doctor's appointment." And she'd been too nervous before it, and too upset after, to face more than a glass of milk.

"Crazy woman. You need to take better care of yourself. How did the appointment go?"

It felt nice to be fussed over and for a second she toyed with telling him about the ultrasound and the decision she had to make. She longed for someone to commiserate with her over the dilemma she was facing.

But what if he told her she was crazy to even consider having a child that might be born with Downs?

Could she handle that?

They were at the café now, *Gloria and Phil's,* a small owner operated place with two tables out front and a few more inside. Eliot checked the menu posted by the open door. "Want a wrap?"

"Too heavy."

"A smoothie? They have a blueberry, banana and yogurt one that sounds looks good."

"Sure."

"Wait out here."

She wasn't too tired to stand in line for her own smoothie. But Dani decided that she would play the pregnancy card and sit for a bit. There was a teenaged couple at the other table, side-by-side, with their legs and shoulders touching. On the table beside them were lattes in tall glass mugs, but they seemed more interested in one another than their beverages.

They looked like they were totally into one another.

And she couldn't help envying them, because they were so young and she could remember what being in love had felt like at that age. Crazy and limitless and absolutely sublime.

"Here we go." Eliot was back, with two take-out glasses filled to the brim. "Want to stay here while we drink these?"

"No. I feel chilly when I'm not moving. Let's keep walking."

The smoothie tasted so wonderful she had to discipline herself from draining it in a flash. "This is what I needed. Thanks."

"You have to get used to eating for two."

"One of the perks of being pregnant." But she didn't want to gain *too* much weight. Also, the literature she'd read had warned against eating excessive amounts of sugar.

"So, have you told your family about the baby?"

"No."

"But you will soon?"

"I suppose."

Eliot gave her an assessing look. "You don't think your sisters are going to judge you because you're not married?"

"Of course not. But I'd hoped to at least be at the stage where I could bring Adrian home to meet them."

"Why don't you ask him?"

She just shook her head. She didn't need to ask, to know Adrian would say no to that idea.

They walked a few more paces, before Eliot suddenly swore. "Why do you put up with his shit? You deserve a hell of a lot better."

The explosion of anger caught her by surprise and made her angry, too. "Just shut up about Adrian, would you?"

"But—"

"No more," she insisted. "I knew when I got into this relationship that it wouldn't be easy. Relationships among the faculty aren't exactly firing offences, but they aren't encouraged either. Adrian's tenured. I'm not. The reason he's so careful to keep our relationship quiet is to protect me, not him."

"And you won't be tenured for what—another four years? Is that how old your child will have to be before Adrian acknowledges that it's his?"

A traffic light turned red, just as Dani was about to cross the street. Eliot grabbed her shoulder and pulled her back. She knew he was just watching out for her, but it seemed that he'd been a bit rougher than he needed to be.

"Why are you so angry?"

He hesitated. Glanced away from her, then back, meeting her gaze squarely. "I care about you, Dani."

"And I appreciate that. You're a good friend. But you have to trust me to know what I'm doing. Adrian—he's going to be there for me. It's just—he's had a lot to go through. With his wife dying, and then, the move. And now getting used to being a single father…"

The light turned green and they were able to cross. Dani could see their condo building just a few blocks ahead.

But she was still thinking about Adrian. "I wish he would talk to me about his wife. But he never even mentions her."

She could feel Eliot grow tense. But he didn't say anything. He did, however, hurl his half-finished smoothie into a trash can as they passed by.

She stopped and stared at him. "What is *with* you today?"

"I just can't handle it anymore."

"Handle what?"

"You. Adrian. This sick relationship you've got yourself messed up in."

"Okay. We have some problems. But it is *not* a sick relationship. That's a really low blow."

"Come on, Dani. You're the one with the psychology degree. Can't you see why he doesn't talk to you about his dead wife?"

Dani took a backward step. Suddenly she wasn't just angry—she was scared. This wasn't like Eliot. Eliot didn't do serious. Eliot did funny and charming and sometime, when provoked, he did sarcastic.

But never serious.

"A lot of men internalize their emotions when they go through a loss."

"Yup. And a lot of them try to numb the pain by seeking out pleasure from another source. The phrase I've heard is, an emotional crutch."

"That's what you think I am? Just a source of pleasure to

numb the pain he feels at losing his wife?" She'd been aware of Eliot's low opinion of her relationship with Adrian. But she'd had no idea he saw her as such a—pitiful figure. "Adrian and I have a real *connection*. You don't have a *clue*."

"Maybe I don't. But I'm not the only clueless one here."

The stubborn, angry expression on his face was one she didn't even recognize. What had happened to the man that she'd thought was her friend?

"So now I'm clueless, huh? Great. Thanks for the free assessment. You'll understand if I don't hang around for any more of your analysis today. In fact, I'm not sure if I ever want to talk to you, again. You should try sticking to the law, Eliot. Something you're actually *trained* to do."

She took off running then, more surprised than relieved when Eliot didn't try to follow. And then, when she was almost at the front door, a sob choked out of her throat, and suddenly she was crying.

That idiot. She fumbled with the key, then hurried inside the lobby. Just for a second she glanced back out at the street, but she couldn't see Eliot anymore. She had no idea where he'd disappeared to, and she told herself she didn't care.

☞ ☜

THE DAY DIDN'T get better. Adrian had to put off their plans for a Thai dinner when Ava came down with a spring cold. And on Friday night, after turning down Miriam's invitation to join her and Eliot for a movie, Dani felt more alone than ever.

Perhaps, she should have agreed to go to that movie. But she still hadn't forgiven Eliot for what he'd said after their run. Frankly, she'd been expecting an apology and could hardly believe he still hadn't offered her one.

She ordered a pizza for dinner, assuaging her guilt by eating it with a glass of milk and handful of baby carrots. When she was done, she tried phoning the Circle C, hoping to speak to Callan. But she'd forgotten her baby sister's penchant for hanging out at Grey's Saloon on Friday nights and got her father instead.

"Hi Dad. How are you? It's Dani," she added, because she knew that she and Callan sounded similar on the phone.

"Good. You?"

If she'd had a different kind of father, Dani might have broken down right then and confessed everything. But as a little girl she'd learned it didn't pay to take her troubles to her father. "I'm good, too. Has the snow melted yet?"

Spring arrived a lot later in Montana than it did in Seattle. From experience she knew the trees wouldn't even start budding for another week or two.

"Still lots up in the mountains."

"How's calving going?"

"Pretty much done now."

The line went silent as she ran out of questions.

"I'll tell your sister you called," Hawksley said. And then he hung up.

She tried calling Sage next, but ended up leaving a message. Of course, she was probably busy with the cowboy who'd come courting her at the Copper Mountain Rodeo last fall. Dawson O'Dell was now a Deputy Sheriff in Marietta, living in a cute house on Bramble Lane with his young daughter Savannah. Dani didn't expect it would be much longer until Sage was living there, too.

When she thought about all the things Dawson had done in order to win Sage's heart—he'd untangled himself from an unhealthy marriage, given up the rodeo, taken community college classes and moved to Marietta—she felt even worse about her relationship with Adrian.

Despite their six months as lovers, she'd never been invited to his home or introduced to his daughter. At work they had to pretend they were only colleagues. And even when she suggested introducing him to Miriam and Eliot, he'd balked.

It was like he'd relegated their relationship to a glass bubble that existed within his world but wasn't really a part of it.

Only now, she was pregnant. And this baby—if she kept it—was going to cause that glass bubble to break.

Dani stared morosely out the window, but since it was now dark all she saw was her reflection gazing back at her. She had no answers. So she went to the sofa, drew up a soft blanket, and then turned on the TV.

An hour later, she was asleep, and didn't wake up until the next morning. She went about her usual weekend chores, half expecting that Eliot would stick a note under the door, maybe suggest a run or Sunday brunch.

But she didn't hear from him or Miriam all weekend.

On Sunday, Portia arrived at six. Not wanting to hurt

her niece's feelings Dani tried not to let on that she'd totally forgotten about their dinner plans.

"Hi honey, do you like Vietnamese? I was thinking of ordering in. Where's Austin?"

"Sure, Vietnamese is good. And Austin is doing final edits on his paper. But he said to thank you for the invitation." Portia looked absolutely adorable in worn jeans, a peach sweater and a pair of funky boots which she took off at the door.

While Dani ordered their meal off the Internet, Portia went to the bank of windows, and sighed. "Mom is always raving about the view at our ranch. But this is so much better."

"I guess if you hadn't grown up around the mountains and Flathead Lake, you might side more with your mother."

"Maybe. Poor Mom might not have that view much longer. Dad wants to sell Bishop Stables."

Dani had been afraid of something like this. Besides her daughters, Mattie lived for the Tennessee Walking horses she and her husband had been raising and training since they married. How would her older sister cope if Wes went through with the divorce and sold the property?

"I hope it doesn't come to that."

Portia shrugged. "I don't think Dad ever really liked the family business. Wren says that's why he kept at the rodeo for so long."

"He's working at a lumberyard in Billings now, though, isn't he?"

"Yeah. And he seems to like it. Oh, I almost forgot. I

bought a bottle of wine." Portia went to the foyer when she'd left a backpack next to her boots. She pulled out a white viognier that she must have noticed Dani serve before. It was one of her favorites.

"That's so sweet. But how did you get it?"

"Austin's twenty-one. He picked it up for me."

Dani had been debating about whether to tell Portia her news. She didn't want to. She hadn't even decided if she was keeping the baby. But she had to give her niece an explanation for not opening the wine.

"I'm going to have to save that bottle. I have some news. It was a surprise to me and it's probably going to be an even bigger one to you."

She could tell by Portia's face that she didn't have a clue where this was heading.

"I've been seeing a man for about six months now. You haven't met him because we work together and we've been keeping our relationship quiet."

"Is that the surprise?" Portia settled on a stool, next to her aunt. "Is he coming for dinner?"

"No." *If only.* "The surprise is that I'm pregnant. It wasn't planned and—" She hesitated, not sure how Portia was going to react. "I still haven't decided if I'm carrying the baby to term."

"Oh. *Oh.*"

Dani sighed. "I guess I'm a living example of everything your mother warned you against."

"Drugs and alcohol were pretty high on her list too."

"Well, I don't use drugs. I'm probably not the best example when it comes to alcohol though, since you know I enjoy my white wine." Her sister Mattie almost never drank, a decision she'd made after a girl she'd once given riding lessons to, Neve Shepherd, got drunk and ended up drowning at a prom after-party. The accident was something Dani remembered well, since Neve had been just two years ahead of her in high school and the entire student body had been traumatized by the event.

"We learned at school and from Mom that no method of birth control is one-hundred percent reliable."

Dani nodded, glad to let her niece assume this was what had happened in her case. "That's very true. And now I'm going to have to ask a favor of you. Do you think you can keep this a secret between us? I haven't told any of the family yet. Partly because I'm not sure I can keep the baby."

"I won't tell," Portia promised. "At least no one in the family. But can I tell Austin?"

"Why not? He's going to be able to see for himself that I'm pregnant soon enough."

Dani realized she was talking as if she was going to keep the baby. But the news from the ultrasound and the decision her doctor expected her to make in the next day or two, still weighed heavily on her mind. It wasn't the sort of quandary she wanted to share with her niece. So as usual, she kept her worries to herself as she got out dishes and poured them glasses of sparkling water in preparation for the meal that would be arriving shortly.

As she moved about her efficient U-shaped kitchen, she could sense Portia watching her. Finally she stopped and lifted her shirt so Portia could see her little belly. "I'm not showing much yet. But soon I'm going to be trending toward blimp status."

Portia giggled. "When is it due? I mean—if you decide to keep it?" Her eyes were big and yearning, and Dani could tell that in her mind her niece was already picturing the addition of an adorable little baby to the family.

But would she be so excited if she knew the baby might have Down Syndrome?

"Second week in September."

"Wow. That's a long time from now."

Dani nodded. In one way it did seem like a long time. But when she considered that almost everything in her life was set to change—it didn't seem nearly long enough.

May

MARVELOUS THINGS STARTED happening in Dani's body in May. As her baby bump pushed out, she began to feel the fluttering motions of the fetus inside. She pictured her baby floating in the amniotic sac like an astronaut in space. When she was alone, she talked to the baby and sometimes sang songs she remembered her mother singing to Callan when she was born. Suddenly, she felt energetic and was never nauseous. Her buoyant good health seemed to her to be an omen. Nothing was wrong with her baby and she refused to allow negative thoughts to spoil this magical time.

Because she loved being pregnant. The changes in her body were beautiful to her. She kept to a strict, healthy balanced diet and the nutritious food seemed to be picking up her mood as well. She'd expecting to crave ice cream and pickles, or other inexplicably weird food combinations. Instead, she ate her way through pints of luscious blueberries and cherries, creamy tubs of yogurt and batch after batch of crispy baked kale.

The word was out at work—though the father hadn't been named. Dani was sure her colleagues were speculating, but only Jenna had dared to ask.

"Someone I've been seeing for about six months," Dani had answered. "The baby wasn't part of our plans, obviously, and we're still trying to work things out."

Jenna, who was older, and had made it clear that neither marriage nor children were in her future, looked puzzled but hadn't commented further. Dani supposed that she, too, wondered why Dani was going through with this pregnancy. She was grateful that Jenna hadn't actually asked the question, because she was tired of trying to explain.

She still hadn't called home with her news for the same reason. Her sisters would grill her, and she just wasn't up to that. Day to day was her new motto.

On Mother's Day, Dani and her sisters connected via Skype, all four of them at the same time. They'd started the tradition the year after their mother's death, back when Mattie was twenty-one, Dani sixteen, Sage twelve and Callan only eight. They'd been at such different stages back then. Mattie had been married and a new mother herself, Dani in High School had been making plans to leave home when suddenly she was in charge of looking after her younger sisters. Sage had still been so young—Callan even younger. They'd had the least time with their mother, but it couldn't be helped. It was sink or swim for the Carrigan girls, and somehow they'd all managed to swim.

Dani set her computer on the dining room table, so only her upper shoulders and face were captured by the camera. On her screen she could see Sage was in the backroom kitchen at her chocolate shop, red hair tied back, and an apron covering her long lean torso. Mattie, looking too thin, but lovely in a gray sweater and jeans was on the sofa by the fireplace in her home at Bishop Stables, while petite, but tough, Callan was in her bedroom at the Circle C, sorting laundry into piles on her bed, and wearing a thin tank top and flannel pajama bottoms.

"How's the weather in Seattle?" Callan wanted to know. She was always preoccupied with the weather—most ranchers were. "We've had a cold, wet spring. Even had snow last week, though most of it has melted now."

"It's beautiful this week," Dani said, biting back the impulse to invite her sisters for a visit. This was the first year none of them had made it to Seattle in time to see the spring blossoms, and she knew it was because they all had things going on in their own lives that made travel difficult. But she was just as happy.

A visit from one of her sisters would mean all of the extended family and the town of Marietta finding out she was pregnant—and Dani didn't want that.

At least, not yet.

But she did enjoy connecting with her sisters, even if not all of the news was good. Mattie's marriage seemed to be truly over. Callan felt their father's health was getting worse, but he refused to book an appointment with a doctor.

Only Sage seemed truly happy. Her relationship with Dawson O'Dell was going well and she got along well with his daughter, Savannah. "There've been a bunch of weddings happening in Marietta, what with the Big Wedding Giveaway and all," Sage added.

"Yes. Callan told me about that." It seemed one of the

Sheenan boys had come up with a PR stunt of paying for one couple's dream wedding, and half the town had entered into the contest.

"Well, Dawson and I have decided we're going to tie the knot too."

"You didn't win the contest, did you?"

Sage laughed. "No. We're thinking of having our wedding after homecoming weekend. The town will have settled down by then and we can keep things easy and low-key."

"I'm happy for you Sage," Mattie said. "Do you want a church wedding? And a catered dinner and dance after?"

"We were thinking of having a smallish affair. At the ranch," Sage said. "What do you think Callan? Would that be too stressful for Dad? Not that we'd expect him to do any of the work."

"It's a great idea," Callan said. "I'll run it by Dad. But since he approves of Dawson it shouldn't be a problem."

"When did he start approving of Dawson?" Last Dani had heard, he'd given Dawson a hard time during the fall round-up.

"On his days off, Dawson often comes out to give us a hand. This spring he's training a new colt dad thinks has some potential. Dad doesn't want to admit it, but he's too old to do that kind of work now. Doesn't stop him from shouting pointers from the sidelines, of course."

Dani could imagine. One of the reasons she'd hated helping with the cattle and horses when she was younger was because of her father's gruff ways and his quick temper when you did something wrong.

Which in her case had seemed to be very often.

"We don't want to have a big wedding party," Sage said. "But I do need a maid of honor. You know I love all of you, so I was thinking of just putting your names in a hat and choosing that way? Sound fair?"

"I appreciate the offer honey, but don't put my name in," Mattie said. "I've been married, raised two daughters and now I'm getting divorced...I'm so happy for you, really I am. But I don't feel like standing up for a wedding at this point in my life."

"I get it." Sage tore two pieces off the end of a sheet of blank paper. "So I'll just put in Dani and Callan's names."

Her baby would be only about a month old by the wedding date. Dani wasn't even sure she'd be able to attend. "Oh, let Callan be the one. She's the baby of the family. Plus, you can shop for dresses together."

"That's a good point. Callan, what do you say?"

"Well, sure. I'd be honored. But—do I really have to wear a dress?"

❧ ❦

Dani lost all track of time at the lab that Monday. She and Jenna were starting a new clinical trial in their quest to determine at what age young children developed a sense of fairness. In this test they would be focusing on whether babies preferred to play with caregivers who distributed toys fairly among a group of children, unfairly in a way that disadvantaged them, or fairly in a way that advantaged them.

The tests took place in little rooms outfitted with a sofa

and three chairs. The three mothers sat behind their babies, with instructions not to interfere unless their child needed comforting. Meanwhile two assistants would offer the babies toys according to a prescribed protocol. From behind one-way glass, Dani and Jenna alternated watching and recording the results at each step of the process.

The work was meticulous and somewhat tedious, but Dani found it fascinating to see the results. It was especially gratifying when they turned out to be similar to what she and Jenna had predicted.

At three o'clock, when the experimenting ended for the day—many of the participating families had to pick up their older children from school at this time—Dani rose from the desk and stretched out her arms. She was awfully tight in her back and shoulders. Maybe tonight she should try to catch a yoga class. She should call Miriam and see if she wanted to come, too. Things had been awkward between them since she and Eliot had that fight.

She still wasn't speaking with him, though her anger had dissipated somewhat. She was almost ready to forgive him now. But the stubborn ass still hadn't asked her to.

"Dani, do you have a minute?" Jenna was at the door, hair pulled back in a tight ponytail and her dark-framed glasses giving her a serious, academic look.

"Sure." Dani saved her spreadsheet, then closed down the laptop.

Jenna waved her into her office, down the hall. For the first thirty minutes they discussed that day's results and whether any modifications to the test would be needed.

It was a positive discussion, but at the end of it, Jenna asked if she could stay a few more minutes. "I'm just wondering what sort of commitment you're going to have to this research after you have the baby?"

Dani was relieved to finally have the subject raised. She valued her work her very much and it was important that Jenna continued to want to work with her. "I intend to keep working until the second week in August."

Jenna nodded, pushing her glasses higher up the bridge of her nose and frowning slightly. "And then?"

"I'd like to take three months off to adjust to the new routine after the birth. And then I was hoping to gradually ease back into all my responsibilities."

"So—part-time at first?"

"If that's okay with you." Jenna's serious demeanor was making her nervous. Legally she couldn't be fired because she was having a baby. But she could be reassigned to less compelling work. And that was something that would be extremely disappointing.

Fortunately, however, that wasn't what Jenna had in mind.

"I think we can make this work. As long as I know your eventual plan is to return full time."

"Within a year, yes."

Jenna nodded. "Good." Bending her head back over her papers, she made it clear that the conversation was over.

Dani left the office feeling only a little relieved. Her job here in the lab with Jenna seemed to be secure. But she couldn't help feeling the senior researcher was disappointed in her decision to have this baby. Jenna was one of those intense, focused people who lived for their work and couldn't understand why other people didn't share the same passion and drive. Once Dani had thought she was that sort of person, too.

But finding out she was pregnant had changed her priorities. She was as surprised as anyone else by how much she wanted this baby. From the moment she'd seen the results of her pregnancy test—at home in the bathroom, worried about her late period—her values and priorities had undergone a massive restructuring.

And there was no going back to the woman she had once been.

~ ~

IT TOOK ABOUT three weeks for Lizbeth Greenway to convince her husband to come in to see Eliot. Nick finally agreed on the condition that he meet with Eliot alone. On the Wednesday he was due to come in, for the last appointment of the day at five o'clock, Eliot took his assistant Paige aside and explained what he needed.

"I want this guy feeling comfortable and unthreatened. So set us up in the Sequoia Room, okay?" The Sequoia Room was more like a large living room area than a conference room. They generally used it for relaxed partner meetings and celebrations. Only rarely for the clients.

"Have a selection of beer there, as well as soft drinks. Maybe even a bowl of potato chips. It's the end of the day, he may feel like unwinding, which is good. Might help me figure out what's going on in his head."

"You're trying to fix the marriage again, aren't you?" Paige was in a lemon-colored dress today, paired with red shoes and a necklace made from what looked like giant, flattened red rocks. Outrageous and sweet all at the same time.

"The wife is pregnant," he shrugged. "I want them to be sure they're taking the right step here."

Paige looked up from her notebook, clearly fighting a smile. "You want to know why I love working for you?"

"Glad to hear that you do."

"Absolutely. For one thing, you never hit on me."

He felt appalled. "You're, like, ten years younger than I am."

"So sweet that you think that way. I've had passes from bosses thirty years older than I am."

In all honesty, he wasn't surprised. He heard things.

"But mostly I love the way you care about people. It's kind of rare in this world."

Again he had to shrug. "I never set out to be a divorce attorney." It had just sort of happened. He'd been given a few cases to handle and they'd gone well, so recommendations had been made, and soon the clients were coming at him like raindrops in a Seattle winter. "Divorce is such a brutal step. I figure if I can keep a few couples out of the fighting ring, that's a good thing."

Paige smiled. "And that's why I love working for you. Leave everything to me. I'll make sure the Sequoia Room is perfect for your meeting."

And it was. At five o'clock when he invited Nick Greenway into the generously proportioned, but still cozy room, he found cushions plumped on the sofa and loveseats. A bowl of potato chips on one side table, some peanuts on another. In the fridge, he found the required beverages, and then some.

"Care for a drink?" he asked his client, rattling off some choices.

Nick looked surprised. In a good way. "I'd love a Pike."

Eliot opened two, then carried them to the window where Nick was standing, looking out at the view. The other man stood at about five nine. He wasn't heavy but you could tell from his body shape that he spent a lot of time at a desk. With his even features, thin brown hair and wire-framed glasses, he'd never stand out in a crowd in either a positive or negative way.

But Nick hadn't needed good looks to get ahead in the world.

He'd used his brain. And teamwork. And the combination had netted him a multi-million dollar company.

Eliot wondered which Nick valued more. The company, or Lizbeth?

After they'd taken their first swallows of the beverage, Eliot went straight to business.

"I'm glad you came, Nick. I hear you're going through a stressful time."

"To be honest, Lizbeth badgered me into coming. Don't see the point, myself. If we're getting divorced, might as well try to make it as quick and painless as possible."

"I'm not sure that's possible. A jointly-owned, multi-million dollar company, makes splitting the assets tricky. Add to that the fact that you'll soon be parents. Well. That's pretty complicated, Nick."

"Not the way I see things." Nick stepped away from the window and gravitated to the sofa closest to the bowl of potato chips. "Mind if I make myself comfortable?"

"Go ahead." That was the idea. Eliot sat in a chair at a ninety-degree angle from Nick, waiting as the other man sampled the chips, then took another drink of beer.

"Lizbeth and I each have completely different roles in the company. We can split the shares fifty-fifty and keep working as usual. Most days we hardly see one another."

"Does she want to keep working full-time after the baby is born?"

Nick glanced away. Eliot guessed he hadn't thought that far ahead.

"As for the baby," Nick finally continued. "Since I'm not the father, it doesn't really matter."

"You sound awfully sure about that."

"Because I am." Nick met his gaze with full on confidence.

When Nick met his gaze with full-on confidence, Eliot felt his control over the situation slipping.

"Your wife sounded pretty sure that you were when I spoke with her."

"Yeah. Funny thing that. She's quite the poker player, my wife. Unfortunately she has no idea that I had myself snipped five years ago." Nick took another drink. "So take your pick. Immaculate conception or an affair. Which do you think my wife has managed to pull off?"

✑ ✑

AT DANI'S MID-MAY check-up with her OB, Dr. Wong seemed pleased. The doctor didn't mention the ultrasound results again, or Dani's failure to call her office and request the amniocentesis, though she did ask, "Should I assume you choose to forego any further diagnostic testing?"

Dani hesitated for a second before nodding.

The truth was, she hadn't made a conscious decision on the matter. She'd simply avoiding calling back the office and booking the test. The way she was behaving was classic denial.

Even knowing that, Dani couldn't make herself think calmly and rationally about the possibility of a chromosomal abnormality. She hadn't told a single soul about the ultrasound findings, either.

Not even Adrian.

They were seeing each other just once a week now, dinner on Wednesdays. They hadn't made love since she'd told him she was pregnant. There was no reason to abstain. Her doctor, and all the literature, made it clear that sex was safe, would not cause harm to the baby.

Dani longed to have Adrian kiss her newly voluptuous breasts, and make love to her passionately, like always. She also craved the quiet cuddling that came after. In her mind she pictured Adrian's hand running over her belly as he talked to the baby—*This is your Daddy*—

But every week Adrian had a new excuse for why he

couldn't come back to her condo. Either he was preparing for a conference, or Ava had a cold, or the live-in nanny had to go out and he needed to be home early.

He showed his love in other ways though. Every week he sent her a gift with a cute card attached. *Flowers for a Woman in Bloom. Cookies for your cravings. Mixed-chocolates for the Mom-to-be.*

But she still yearned for his touch.

This week, hopefully, it would happen. After work on Wednesday Dani put on a lacy bra and the new dress she'd bought to make the most of her cleavage. There were advantages to being pregnant and tonight she intended to put them on display.

She took a cab to the restaurant where they'd arranged to meet, hoping after their meal Adrian would give her a ride home. Then she'd invite him in and they'd end up in bed together.

The early evening sun was warm on her bare shoulders when she stepped out of the taxi twenty minutes later. A sweet taste of the summer to come. Two beautiful spring flower arrangements flanked the front door to Bonterra Bistro, inviting her to step inside, but first she checked up and down the street for Adrian.

She didn't see him. So she made her way inside on her own, hoping that for once she'd find him waiting for her at their table.

But he was late. As usual.

She passed the time studying the menu, then checking e-mail messages on her phone.

It would have been easy to feel annoyed. Instead, she took deep, calming breaths, reminding herself that they had all night. She had big plans for the evening and didn't want to start out feeling peeved.

When he finally came in, he looked like he'd just woken up from a nap, his dark curly hair wind-blown despite the calm day and the t-shirt under his open jacket rumpled. Despite his unkempt appearance, she felt the usual rush of pleasure at the sight of him.

When their gazes connected, she felt it again, a wonderful zapping of warmth spreading out from her heart.

"I'm sorry," he muttered. "The damn nanny—"

He stopped at her chair to give her a chaste kiss and as he drew back she noted with satisfaction that his gaze drifted to her voluptuous cleavage.

And lingered.

After the server came and took their orders, she leaned in closer to him, watching again as his eyes slipped from her face, to her breasts, then back again.

"So—what was the problem with the nanny?"

"It's not really her fault, I guess. It's always hard breaking in a new one."

Only when he said that did Dani remember that he'd had to let his old nanny go because she kept spending her evenings out with her friends and her sister—rather than in the private suite attached to the back of Adrian's house. Then the next morning, she'd show up late for work.

Dani knew the layout of Adrian's house because she'd been there once when Ava was on a playdate and their affair was new and hot and exciting. She would have taken a closer look if she'd realized then that she wouldn't be invited back a second time.

The new nanny—Olga?—had only been on the job for two weeks.

"I'd planned to come here straight from work," Adrian continued. "But she was trying to put on a TV show for Ava and had forgotten how to switch the input mode from Apple TV to cable. So I had to swing by the house. And then Ava didn't want me to leave."

He brushed a hand though his tangled curls, drawing attention to just how thick and wonderful his hair was. A hint of stubble defined the contours of his high cheekbones and well defined jaw and chin.

If Adrian had a physical flaw, it was probably his fitness level and the presence of ten extra pounds around his middle. But as a working dad he claimed he had no time to hit the gym, and Dani couldn't fault him for that. She'd rather he spend all his extra time with *her* than the treadmill any day.

He asked about her research after their meals were served, several times setting down his cutlery and leaning in, his small, brown-as-mahogany eyes watching her intently as she spoke. He made her feel like everything she said was absolutely fascinating. This was what had drawn them together in the first place. Their love of research and their work.

Then she asked about his project, analyzing data from an ongoing study on the effect of video games on the academic and athletic success of tens of thousands of boys and girls from across the country. So far Adrian had published two papers on the subject and was earning a reputation as one of the leading experts in the area.

They could have talked for hours more, but when the bill came she remembered her strategy to seduce Adrian tonight if it killed her. She pulled out her lip-gloss and freshened her makeup with slow, deliberate strokes of the wand against her lips. It worked. She could feel the heat building between them, and she stoked it higher when she slipped one foot from her shoe and ran it up the length of his calf.

"I took a cab. Will you give me a lift home?"

From his expressive mouth and eyes she could see he was feeling desire—but battling it.

He signed the check, tucked his wallet back inside his coat pocket. "Of course I'll give you a lift. But I can't come in. The nanny is too new…"

"I'm sure she'll phone you if she has any trouble." Dani stood, letting the strategic folds of her dress camouflage her tummy, while highlighting her newly ample cleavage. When Adrian stood up beside her, she slipped her hand into his and moved closer. "I miss you. It's been a long time—"

He swallowed. Weakening against whatever resolve he'd erected between them. Outside Adrian placed a hand on the small of her back as he guided her to his parking space. It was almost dark now, and the city had the settling in feeling that comes when shops close and people head home to prepare for another workday the next morning.

As she got into the passenger seat, Dani could sense

Adrian checking out her legs. One part of her body that was so far untouched by the pregnancy. They drove in a sweet silence that, for Dani, at least, was filled with anticipation. She hoped Adrian was thinking about taking her to bed. Stripping her clothes and making sweet love together.

At the condo, he pulled into a parking stall for visitors and walked her to the door.

She was certain he intended to come inside. But all he did was kiss her gently and tell her good night.

She took hold of his hands. "What's going on?" She realized she had to be more specific. This limbo between them had to end. Trying to prepare herself for the worst she asked, "Do you want to end things between us?

His "No," sounded perfunctory.

"Are you sure? Because a platonic relationship isn't of interest to me. And it wasn't what you used to want either."

"I still find you beautiful. Very desirable. I just—don't want to hurt you."

Was he talking about physically? "What hurts is thinking you don't want me anymore."

"As if that was even possible." He ran his hands down her bare arms, then pulled her in close for a kiss. It started tenderly, then quickly grew deep and full of need.

They were inside and on the elevator in under a minute, and finding themselves alone, they kissed again. Adrian held back her hair so he could have access to the side of her neck, one of her favorite hot spots. And then his hands were working their way up, gently cupping her breasts through the silky fabric of her dress and the lacy barrier of the bra.

"Do they hurt?" He whispered the question in her ear, where his hot breath gave her a shiver of pleasure.

His question reminded her that this was a man who understood the changes pregnancy caused in a woman's body. "No. Not anymore."

But then the elevator doors opened and they had to make their way across the hall and she had to find her key, unlock the door, all the while hoping that neither Miriam or Eliot—or any of the other residents on this floor, would suddenly appear to break the mood.

They didn't.

And soon she and Adrian were inside, in her bedroom, where Adrian kissed her again, then slowly unzipped the back of her dress, until it fell to her waist. He brushed his hands over her breasts, still held firm in the bra. He kissed the deep valley between them, then slowly released the catch.

And groaned. "Oh, baby."

They made love fast and furious, not quite managing to shed all of their clothes, only the ones that were completely necessary—her panties. His pants.

Dani's orgasm came fast, soared high, then left her quickly. She held onto Adrian's shoulders, wanting to keep the buzz alive for a little longer. But then he was coming, too, with a desperate panting, then a groan.

"Oh, baby."

He only ever called her that when they were making love. He rolled onto his back, keeping hold of her hand, so they were both staring up at the ceiling when he asked again.

"You're sure I didn't hurt you?"

"God, no." She laughed, before it occurred to her that she was being insensitive. "Adrian, how far along was your wife when she died?"

For almost a minute all she could hear was the sound of him breathing. Then, quietly, he said, "Four months."

She'd been killed in a car crash. Ava, buckled into a car seat in the back hadn't had a scratch. The baby in Vanessa's womb hadn't had a chance.

Dani thought about her own baby. She put a hand on her belly, wishing Adrian would do the same. Didn't he want to feel the presence that was his child? But he was already cleaning himself, handing her a tissue.

"Come back to bed," she said, trying not to sound like she was pleading. "Let's get under the covers and cuddle for a bit.

Whenever Vanessa was mentioned, he always clammed up. She wanted him to talk to her about his wife. There should be no off-limits topic between them.

"I really can't. I promised the new nanny I wouldn't be late."

"I'm sure she's fine. And Ava is probably asleep by now." Even as she was speaking the words, Dani realized she was sounding like a mistress, trying to convince her married lover to spend the night. It was unsettling, distasteful.

Feeling suddenly exposed and vulnerable in her half-naked state, she scrambled into her yoga clothes which were laid out on a nearby chair. By the time she was dressed, Adrian had returned from the washroom, his face damp, and his hair somewhat neater.

He sat on the bed and patted the spot beside him.

"I think we should talk."

This was all wrong. She settled next to him, unhappily. They were supposed to be naked, in one another's arms, under the covers. He was supposed to be opening up to her about his worries and fears, his hopes for the future—for *their* future.

"I was right earlier." She could hear how flat her voice sounded. "You *do* want to end things."

He sighed. "No. What I wanted was to keep things as they were."

"I didn't *plan* on getting pregnant."

"No. But you did make the choice to keep the baby. And while I respect your right to make that choice, my position hasn't changed. And it won't."

Dani folded her arms protectively over her midsection. Not once all evening had he allowed his gaze or his hands to go anywhere near the place on her body where their baby was growing. She hadn't needed to hear him speak these words to know he still didn't want her to have this child. *Their* child.

"I haven't asked you for anything, Adrian. And I won't."

"You haven't asked. But I see the hope in your eyes every time we're together. And I'm sorry, darling, but it isn't going to happen. I'm not at a point where I'm ready to get married again. It takes everything I have to be a good dad to Ava."

"Okay. But what about a year from now? Two years?"

"I wish I could promise you I'd feel differently by then. But how can I?"

Dani stared down at her hands, twisted together in her

lap. "So where does that leave us?"

"It's your decision as much as mine. I feel we should tone things down. I want to support you in the months to come. And later, when the baby's here—that support should become financial in nature."

"I don't want your money."

"Maybe not. But I have an obligation to the child. I don't want to make you feel like this is a business transaction or something, but I think it's smart to get a lawyer involved."

She felt as if he'd slapped her. "I'm not your adversary."

"I just want to make sure I'm treating you and the baby fairly."

"Honestly. You don't have to worry about me and the baby. I'm more than capable of providing for both of us."

When he didn't reply, suddenly she understood that this wasn't about his concern for her and the child. It was about covering his ass—legally and professionally. If news ever came out about this, he didn't want to look like the bad guy.

She stood and went to the door. "You should leave now."

"I didn't say those things to hurt you. I want to help."

"Leave, Adrian. Now."

It gave her a mild amount of satisfaction to see that he hadn't expected this reaction, and that it unbalanced him. He fumbled with his belt, then as he passed her on the way to the front door, there was an awkward moment when he tried to kiss her good-bye.

At the door, he gave it one last shot. "I still want to be your friend, Danielle."

"Are you sure that's wise? Maybe you should run that

idea by your lawyer, first."

"Danielle—"

He was the one who was pleading now, but she could also see relief in his eyes. No doubt he'd been worried about this "situation" for some time now and was glad that he'd finally tackled it head on.

Pride wouldn't let her reveal how close she was to breaking down. But she needed him out of here—fast—before it happened. Opening the door, she took his arm and almost tugged him out of her home.

And wouldn't you know it—at just that moment the elevator doors opened and Eliot stepped out. He looked like he was coming home late from the office, or a dinner meeting. Tall and lean in his rumpled, but expensive suit, he looked like a GQ model after a long, exhausting photo shoot.

The two men sized one another up in a second.

Adrian stopped trying to resist her, while Eliot put a hand on the elevator door to keep it from closing.

"Going down?" Eliot asked, his voice hard, his gaze unflinching.

"Yes."

"Good." Eliot didn't remove his hand until the other man was safely inside.

As for Adrian, he didn't give Dani as much as a parting wave or even a glance. Which was just as well, she supposed. She could feel her body trembling now. A delayed reaction to tension.

She tried to give Eliot a brief smile and close the door on

him. But he wouldn't let her get away with that.

"You need tea," he said. "I'll make you some."

"I'd rather be alone."

"Like hell you would." And taking advantage of her open door, he stepped inside.

❧ ❧

AS HE FILLED the kettle with water, Eliot took stock of the situation. Adrian had left looking flustered, dressed in clothing appropriate for work. Dani, on the other hand was in her yoga outfit. Her hair was tangled, her skin was pale, and her hands were trembling.

All the evidence pointed to two things. They'd had sex. Then a fight. It made him feel kind of mad that they'd had the sex. The fight part was good, though.

He opened the cupboard where she stored tea, coffee and all her spices. "What kind of tea do you want?" He peered at the labels. "Green? Mint? Coconut Jasmine?"

"Thanks Eliot. I know you mean well. But I don't want tea." She'd followed him into the kitchen. From one of the drawers she pulled out an old fashioned copper recipe box. He remembered his grandmother owning something similar.

"What are you doing? They have recipes on the Internet now, you know."

"They don't have recipes for Mrs. Bowman's Shepherd pie." Finding the card she needed, she pulled it out, then went to her fridge. From the freezer she pulled out a package of ground beef. "Thaw this in the microwave for me, would you?"

He removed the packaging, found a glass bowl with a lid, and then did as she asked. By the time he was done, Dani was peeling potatoes at the sink. "If you still want to help, you could dice an onion."

"O-kay. But this is a pretty heavy meal for nine o'clock on a Wednesday night." He stopped himself from adding, *Didn't Adrian at least take you out for a decent meal before you jumped in the sack with him?*

Better sense prevailed, because it had been a long time since he and Dani had had a civil conversation. He hadn't regretted the things he'd said to her. But he did miss her. So maybe, this time, he'd be a little more careful how he put things.

"This isn't for us. It's for Mr. Bowman in 806."

Their neighbor was in his mid-seventies, a retired dentist who had moved into the condo building after the renovation, just like the rest of them. "Didn't his wife die last fall?"

"She did. And he really misses her. He misses doing the morning crossword with her, taking their afternoon strolls together. And he really misses her Shepherd pie. Which is why I sometimes make it for him."

"That's nice. But why now? Maybe we could do this on the weekend?"

"Mom always told me, whenever you're feeling sorry for yourself, the best cure is to do something nice for someone else." Dani added water to the potatoes, then put them on to boil.

"So we're making Shephard Pie for Mr. Bowman?"

"So we're making Shephard Pie for Mr. Bowman."

He was going to have to go along with her madness. Because at this point it didn't seem wise to leave her alone in a room with sharp knives. He picked up the recipe card. It was old, with slanted, feminine handwriting and a myriad of unidentifiable food splatters. "This looks complicated."

"It's all about layers." Dani was pulling condiments from her fridge now. Tomato paste and soy sauce and hot mustard. "First layer, ground beef with sautéed onions and homemade barbecue sauce."

He pulled out her biggest frying pan. "Check."

"Second layer, mixed vegetables. The frozen kind, because those are the ones Mrs. Bowman used to use." She opened the freezer and produced such a bag.

"Let me guess the third layer—mashed potatoes?"

She nodded. "Topped with shredded cheese."

"Layers."

"Exactly."

By the time they had the onions sautéed, the ground beef browned and all of it mixed with the homemade barbecue sauce that Dani had whipped up, the potatoes were ready to be mashed, and the cheese had to be grated. In just twenty minutes they had a completed casserole on the counter, waiting to be popped into the oven.

Eliot eyed it approvingly. "You know, I'm starting to feel a little hungry."

"For Mr. Bowman," Dani insisted, covering it with foil then hiding it in her fridge. "It's kind of late. I'll take it to him tomorrow."

Then she stood back and surveyed the mess they'd made

of the kitchen.

"Feeling better?" Eliot asked.

She started to cry.

He'd known it was a matter of time. He'd seen how she was fighting back emotions as she cooked, often blinking rapidly, her lower lip trembling.

"It's not that bad," he said. "I can have this mess cleaned up in ten minutes." He gave it a closer look. "Make that fifteen."

She gave him a weak smile. "Oh, Eliot. You've been so nice tonight. I'm sorry about our fight. Sorry, I got so mad at those things you said."

Not many women looked pretty when they cried. Dani was no exception. But she did look vulnerable. And sweet. He had to fight the urge to hug her. "And I'm sorry I said them."

"You shouldn't be. Because you were right."

Eliot had started loading the dishwasher. But he stopped when she said that. "I think you're ready for that cup of tea now."

She hesitated, then nodded. "In a minute. I need to wash up, first."

As she headed to the washroom, he put the kettle back on, then washed the frying pan and put the pot that had been used to mash the potatoes in to soak. By the time she returned, he had a cup of mint tea ready.

They sat at the sofa, turned, so they faced one-another, Dani with her legs crossed in a yoga position that amazed him.

"I was wrong about Adrian. I thought our relationship was going somewhere. That all he needed was time to see how we belonged together."

Eliot wasn't a violent man. But his hands automatically formed fists as he recalled Adrian scurrying onto that elevator. Why hadn't he smashed-in that guilty, but relieved-looking face when he'd had the chance?

"He told me he was going to contact a lawyer about setting up payments for the baby."

"Well. That's good, right?" At least the scum-bag was accepting some responsibility here.

"I don't care about the money! I can afford a baby, Eliot. What I need is someone to help me raise it. I don't want to be a single mother. Especially if—" She stopped. Shook her head, then took a sip of tea. "I just didn't figure I'd be doing this all on my own. I mean, he already has the responsibility of raising a daughter. He's not like you—living a single and carefree life. I could certainly see why someone like you might balk at the idea of becoming a dad."

Eliot had never thought of himself in the father role. Neither one of his older brothers was married, or had children. Yet hearing Dani dismiss his parenting abilities so quickly, was a little annoying.

"I don't think I'd be an *awful* father."

"That's not what I meant. I'm not trying to insult you. I'm just pointing out that I wasn't expecting the moon from Adrian."

No, not the moon. Just a wedding ring and a settled family life.

"When I first met you, you seemed so career focused. I never would have guessed how much you wanted to start a family."

"I didn't either. Not until I found out I was pregnant." She thought for a moment. "Actually, that isn't true. I think I wanted more from Adrian almost from the start."

Eliot shifted uneasily on the couch. He knew that people often settled for less than they truly wanted out of a relationship. Those were the types of people who ended up in his office. But it wasn't just married people who made the settling mistake.

"I get that you're sad about Adrian. But one thing you shouldn't doubt is your ability to be a single mother. I've known you for two years. And yes, you're smart as hell and sure to go far in your profession. But you also like taking care of things." He thought of the sickly row of plants she'd nurtured so carefully. Mr. Bowman. Hell, even Adrian— hadn't she taken on the grief stricken widower hoping to make him happy again? "You're going to make an excellent mother."

She curled her legs up, hugging her knees in a way her growing middle wouldn't allow her to do for much longer. "Eliot, you're going to make me cry. Admittedly not that difficult to achieve today."

The urge to take her in his arms hit him again. Harder this time.

Hard enough, in fact, to make him wonder how he really felt about his next-door neighbor. If this were Miriam on the couch, crying over some problem in her life, would he feel that same urge?

He didn't think so.

Which meant—maybe it was time for him to leave.

⮞ ⮜

AFTER WORK ON Thursday, Dani delivered the Shepherd's pie to Mr. Bowman and he was very appreciative. So at least something good had come out of her terrible evening with Adrian. Back in her condo, Dani ate a grilled cheese sandwich and followed it up with a cup of herbal tea.

God she missed wine. Coffee, too, and the super dark chocolate she loved.

But most of all, right this minute, she missed wine.

She could hardly believe she'd had the guts to make a final break with Adrian. Already she missed him so much and longed to give him a call.

No. She couldn't let herself backslide like that. Besides, she'd sound so pathetic.

Something else good had happened last night, at least. She and Eliot had made up. Finally. He'd been so sweet to help her with the cooking and cleaning and even letting her cry about Adrian without saying *I told you so.*

But he *had* told her so, and in not-so-much words but the lack of them, so had Miriam.

Yet Dani had gone full throttle into a relationship with a man who right from the start made it clear he wanted to keep her on the back burner.

She felt like such a fool. A classic case, in fact, of a woman who should have read *He's Just Not that into You.*

If only she could understand why he wasn't.

She went through the checklist of reasons Adrian should love her. They had attraction, common interests—and soon, a child. Yet, for him the equation came out incomplete. Something in her was missing, she just didn't know what it was.

Would that same missing thing make her a terrible mother?

Despite Eliot's attempt to be reassuring last night, she was actually terrified about being the sole adult in charge of a child—especially one that might have extra challenges. She'd almost confessed this little secret to Eliot last night, too. What would he have said?

Surely, he would have thought she was an even bigger fool than he already did.

Because she'd had her chance to do extra testing and to take steps if the results were problematic—yet she hadn't. She'd buried her head in the sand after that ultrasound. Much the way she'd avoided the truth about her relationship with Adrian.

And now the consequences were coming.

And they wouldn't just be suffered by her. But by this poor, innocent baby inside her.

June

THOUGH DISASTER WAS approaching on the horizon, in June the days floated by in a pleasant routine of teaching, final exams and interesting developments at the lab. Dani's body continued to blossom and she found herself craving the bounty of fresh cherries for sale at Pike's Market.

Miriam and Eliot continued to support her by inventing ever new virgin cocktails recipes for their get-togethers—which were now happening every Friday without fail. Their support kept Dani from doing anything foolish like calling Adrian and begging him to get back together.

She missed him horribly, but what was hardest to let go of, was her dream of making a family with him. She'd never met Ava, but she ached for the little girl who had lost her mother at such a young age. Dani knew she would have loved Ava like her own—if Adrian had given her the chance.

She supposed now was the time to start adjusting to the idea of being a single mother. It seemed so easy on the *Gilmore Girls*. But Dani didn't have any real life role models to follow. Back in Montana families tended to stick together, even when they weren't very happy. Her own mother had felt trapped in her marriage, Dani knew. So much so that she'd had an affair. But even that affair hadn't ended her marriage to Hawksley. They'd stuck together.

Through thick and thin, sickness and health, riches and poverty—

Her sister, Mattie, was probably one of the first in the family to ever get divorced. But at least her children were college-aged when it happened. Portia and Wren had grown up with a mother and father under the same roof—at least most of the time. Though their father had spent a lot of time on the road, a part-time father was better than no father at all.

Which was what her poor child was going to have.

Time and again Dani considered calling Mattie. Of all her sisters, surely she would be most likely to commiserate and to offer the words of wisdom and guidance that Dani's mother would have given if she were still alive.

But—Dani couldn't.

All her life she'd been the smart one in the family. And now she'd done so many dumb things. Unprotected sex, an affair with an emotionally unavailable man, refusing her screening tests for Downs—

She couldn't keep hiding these mistakes from her sisters.

Sticking her head in the sand—yet again—wouldn't solve anything.

But each day seemed to take everything she had. All her strength, all her courage, all her energy. In the evening when Mattie, Sage and Callan were just a phone call away, Dani made other choices. TV, a book, a slow-paced run to Washington Park Arboretum.

A few times there were phone calls from Adrian. Dani

never answered and deleted the messages without listening to them.

Cold turkey was the only way to handle this.

Fortunately her day-to-day work routine had never involved Adrian and she managed to come up with a good excuse to miss the June faculty meeting so she didn't even see him then.

If he wanted to settle things between them financially with a lawyer, she wouldn't say no. She'd put his money into an educational fund for their child. In the meantime she couldn't handle seeing him or talking to him. She was afraid she'd cry.

Or beg him to come back.

Which only proved how low she'd sunk.

Mid-June Portia finished her Spring Quarter, and Dani drove to the Pi Phi sorority house to pick her up and take her to the airport.

Austin was on hand to see her off, looking very much the young cowboy in jeans, boots and a western-styled shirt. All he was missing was the cowboy hat. He lugged Portia's suitcases out of her room, down to the street, then loaded the biggest into the trunk of the Volvo and jammed the smaller one into the back seat.

Her niece looked totally adorable in a pretty summer dress and wedge sandals, her hair in soft curls around her heart-shaped face. "Thanks, Austin."

"I'm going to miss you."

"You better come and visit then."

"I've already got a few rodeos lined up in Montana," he

promised.

Dani turned and got behind the steering wheel, giving the young couple a few moments for a goodbye kiss. Thirty seconds later, Portia got into the car and Austin closed the door.

"Good to go," Portia said breathlessly.

Dani could see Austin in her rear view mirror, still waving, as she drove away from the sorority house.

"Looking forward to your summer?" she asked once they were on the freeway.

"Sort of. It will be good to see Mom and Wren, and to be home. But it's going to feel different without Dad."

There had been times, growing up, when Dani could have done without having her father around. Times when he'd yelled at her—or worse, made her mother cry. But Wes had been a different kind of dad to the twins. When they were little, he'd give them piggy-back rides and shown them his simple—but to them baffling—magic tricks. Wes wasn't the yelling kind, either, and though he was a tease, never did so with the intention of hurting anyone's feelings.

"I'm sure it will be an adjustment," Dani said diplomatically. "But look at the bright side—no textbooks or pop quizzes!"

Portia laughed. "There's that. I just hope I find a summer job. Mom hasn't said anything, but with the divorce and everything, I get the feeling money is a little tight."

As the exit for the airport loomed, Portia changed the subject. "What about your baby, Aunt Dani? Am I allowed to tell Wren and Mom about it now?"

For the past few months Portia had been the one person who was unequivocally happy about Dani's pregnancy. Dani appreciated that. But she also suspected Portia didn't understand the challenges that would come with the package. Nor did Portia know about the ultrasound and the possibility of complications.

"I know you're close to your Mom and sister. If you feel you have to tell them, it's okay. But I'd really rather keep it quiet a while longer."

"Won't the baby be born in September?"

"Yes."

"So—when are you planning on telling everyone?"

When I know for certain I have a healthy, normal baby. But she couldn't say that. "I've been thinking it might be fun to surprise them. After the baby is born. What do you think?"

"Oh my God."

Dani tightened her grip on the steering wheel. Shot an anxious look at her niece. Expecting to see a shocked expression, instead she was met with a beaming smile.

"That is an *awesome* idea. They are going to be so *blown away.*"

The blown away part was sure to be true. Dani wasn't so sure about the awesome part.

❧ ❦

FOR THE NIGHT of the solstice, Miriam booked the condo's rooftop patio. "Let's watch the sunset and enjoy every minute of the longest day of the year."

"Sounds like a plan," Dani agreed. They'd never celebrated the solstice before. But this seemed like a good year to start, and they did have an awesome patio on the roof of the condo building, complete with handsome teak furniture, a long, concrete gas fireplace and lots of potted cedars to add a touch of nature. Plus the three-hundred and sixty-degree view was pretty spectacular.

Eliot was in, too. He concocted a special drink for the occasion and ordered a tray of samosas with spicy mango dipping sauce.

Up until this night, Dani's friends had been in solidarity with her alcohol-free life—at least on the evenings they spent together. Tonight, however, Miriam brought a bottle of vodka up to the patio and insisted on spiking both her and Eliot's glasses. Within an hour Dani could see the effects of the alcohol on her friends as everything became more relaxed—including their tongues.

"God, this is fun," Miriam said. "I'm so glad summer is here. It's been a hell of a long winter."

Had it, Dani wondered? Compared to what she'd been used to in Montana the rainy days and clouds in Seattle never seemed so intolerable. "Are you taking any holidays?" she asked her friends.

"I'd like to take two weeks. You guys want me to book my family's cottage again?" Eliot offered.

"Oh, yes." Dani had been hoping he'd offer. The three of them had gone to his beach house on the Hood Canal last year for a few days and vowed that next year they'd go for longer.

"I'm in. Assuming I still live here. My parents called me today." Miriam snagged the second to last samosa and dipped one end in the mango sauce. "They're on my case to move back to Vancouver."

"Then who would help me with my shopping?" Dani objected.

"And lead me into temptation?" Eliot added another splash of vodka to his drink.

Dani smiled indulgently. She didn't blame them for kicking back a little tonight. It was amazing, actually, that they'd embraced the whole virgin cocktail thing at all.

"Well. My online career is stagnated. And the whole, marry a rich American plan hasn't exactly worked out either." Miriam dipped the second corner of her samosa in the sauce.

"When's the last time you went on a date?" Dani's own life had been so full of upheaval, she'd kind of lost track of Miriam's. She gave herself a mental kick and made a silent pledge to be a better friend."

"Not since Christmas. I pulled my name out of all the email dating sites. Nothing was working out." Miriam dipped the third, final corner in the sauce and polished off the samosa. When she was done, she sank gloomily into the corner of the L-shaped sectional.

Looking at her, it was hard to believe she couldn't have any man she wanted. She was so pretty, with her slender, petite frame. Dani tended to feel like an Amazon woman when she was around Miriam. Now that she was pregnant the differences between them were only magnified.

"I could introduce you to some of my co-workers," Eliot offered. "And if it doesn't work out, I'll handle your divorce for free."

"Maybe you could handle my marriage, too."

"How so? I'm not a judge, at least not yet." Eliot put down his drink.

"But you could be the groom. It's not as if you're dating anyone seriously."

Eliot gaped. "You're saying *I* should be your Green Card Guy?"

Dani listened to the exchange feeling increasingly uneasy. There was something in the way Miriam was looking at Eliot. Something she'd never noticed before.

Miriam *likes* him. *Really likes him.*

But then Miriam laughed and gave a cavalier toss of her hand. "Hey. It was worth a shot."

And Dani was left wondering if she'd imagined that look of longing in her friend's eyes.

ঙ ৩

TIME, WEEKS AND then months of it, had slipped away since Eliot's last meeting with Lizbeth Greenway. Nothing made that more obvious, than the size of Liz's belly when she showed up early for her June twenty-eighth appointment.

Eliot tried to keep his smile in place as he offered her his hand. She didn't just shake it though. She gripped it tightly, using him as a counterweight as she rose up from the reception room's sofa.

"Four more weeks to go," she said. "I can't tell you how

ready I am for all of this to be over."

All of this being her pregnancy? Or the divorce from Nick?

"Paige has us in the Sequoia Room today." Eliot held the door for her, then pointed out the directions. His client's formerly confident stride was now a wide-legged waddle. Would Dani get that big? That ungainly? He couldn't imagine it.

The efficient Paige had made sure the room was stocked with assorted fruit juices and sparkling waters today. Instead of potato chips and peanuts, there was a veggie tray with hummus and kale chips.

Eliot made sure Lizbeth was comfortable before taking a seat himself. "So how are things going? I take it Nick told you about his—" Eliot hesitated before saying the word— "vasectomy?"

"Yes, he told me. Finally. What kind of man gets himself snipped without first consulting his wife? For years, I thought we were trying to get pregnant. Turns out, it was only me trying. He knew all along it would never happen. Yet, he let me go through all those ups and downs. The hope and the disappointment."

Last time Eliot had seen Lizbeth, she'd looked fashionable and attractive in her pregnant state. Today it seemed as if she'd given up all effort to look good. Her hair was pulled back in a severe bun. And the gray color of her leggings and t-shirt did nothing to flatter her coloring. She'd worn no make-up or jewelry, not even her engagement ring, though she had kept on the wedding band.

She noticed him looking at it. "I'm wearing this to keep rumors quiet at work. A few people have noticed Nick and I aren't driving to and from the office together anymore. But they've put it down to my pregnancy. Needing more sleep, that sort of thing. Although, probably there is some gossip flying. People always notice more than you think they do."

She was, he thought, avoiding the main issue here. Yes, her husband had been deceitful about his vasectomy. But it did rather leave the question of who had fathered her child unanswered. "I'm glad Nick was finally open with you about his vasectomy. Is it safe to assume you reciprocated by being honest about the paternity of your baby?"

She looked annoyed. But she nodded. "It was just a one night thing. Nick had been so distant. And I was away on a business trip. Lonely." She shrugged. "No excuse, I know. But at least my deception was just for one night. Nick's been lying to me for years."

As far as Eliot was concerned, deception was deception. The fact that neither one of them had been honest with each other about such important things told Eliot that this marriage might not be as salvageable as he'd once hoped.

"What about the man—the baby's father? Have you spoken to him?"

"I wasn't going to. But Nick, he insisted. Said he wouldn't come to this meeting unless I did. So, I tracked the guy down and phoned him a few weeks ago. He's married too and not looking for complications. He told me he'd pay support if I wanted. I said no. He said when my child is older, if she or he ever wants to meet him, he'd go along with that. But he doesn't want to be a part of the child's regular life."

Eliot was finding it hard to feel compassion for his client. She seemed so—cold and unremorseful. But the next instant she was crying, covering her face with her hands. He found some tissues, then waited for her to calm down.

"I'm sorry. It's awful, isn't it? I can't believe I did something so stupid. I'd never cheated on Nick before. And I never would have, again. I felt so icky afterward. Really, really icky."

There was a tapping at the door, then. While Lizbeth pulled herself together, Eliot went to the door, waiting as Paige ushered Nick into the room. Unlike his wife, Nick hadn't changed much from the last time Eliot saw him. Except, while his wife had been gaining weight and substance with her baby, Nick had been losing. His suit looked baggy, and his face gaunt.

"Hey, Nick." Eliot shook his hand, then stepped back to allow the married couple to address one another. Their "Hellos" were subdued, and this time Nick refused Eliot's offer of a beverage, instead taking a seat opposite from his wife's.

"Is there anything else I can get you?" Paige asked. Her blonde hair was pulled back in her customary ponytail and she was wearing a cornflower-blue dress, with shoes and jewelry a contrasting, sunshiny yellow.

"No thanks. We're fine for now." He gave her a thankful smile before closing the door behind her.

Nick and Lizbeth were avoiding eye contact. But they

were clearly nervous and on edge around one another. Eliot was hopefully that they were done with yelling stage. It was one of the reasons he'd suggested so many weeks lapse between their meetings. Given the huge revelation Nick had made last time, a cooling-off period had seemed wise.

"Okay," Eliot said. Time to step into the ring. "Thanks for coming. You two have been through some tough months. I like to think you've finally been honest with one another. Because it's always good to have the facts before you make a decision. And divorce is a mighty big decision."

He noticed they both winced when he said *divorce*. A good sign. "You guys know I'm not a marriage counselor. I still think you would both benefit by seeing one, though."

"No way." Nick spoke up immediately. "This is good. We're talking. We're being honest. What more could a counsellor do?"

"Probably a lot more. For one thing, a counselor would probably want you, Nick, to tell Lizbeth why you had that vasectomy without telling her."

Nick rested his forearms on his legs and leaned toward his wife. "You know both my dad and grandfather died of early onset Alzheimers."

She nodded.

"I've always felt fatalistic about my chances of getting it, too. But when you started talking about babies, it got me thinking. I didn't want to bring a child into the world knowing I might pass along the genes for that effing disease."

"Oh, Nick. I wish you'd told me about this."

"And I wish you hadn't slept with some random guy you

met at a conference."

Lizbeth had been leaning forward in her chair, her expression softening and warming. But this last comment from her husband had her physically and emotionally pulling back.

"Right." She snapped back. "I wonder why I strayed, when I was getting so much love and affection from my husband."

"That's what happens when you decide to take a company public. A move you voted in favor of, remember?"

"Hang on," Eliot interrupted. Fortunately they both calmed down immediately and looked at him. He pointed at his chest. "Not a marriage counsellor, remember? You guys need to take this home. And talk."

Nick shook his head. "Oh, what's the point? We all know how this is going to end."

Lizbeth looked as if she was holding her breath, as her husband turned away from her. Nick didn't even say goodbye when he left the room.

Worried about Lizbeth, Eliot offered her a glass of water, but she declined.

"He's angry now." She gathered her purse, then worked her way out of her seat. "But we will talk. Later. When he's cooled down."

Eliot escorted her to the elevators, feeling disheartened. They'd both been deceptive. Never a good thing in a marriage. Despite that, he suspected they still loved one another. The question was whether they could also forgive.

July

"YOU SHOULD HAVE gone for the testing. Found out whether you're having a boy or girl."

Miriam and Dani were in Pottery Barn, trying to decide on a color scheme for the baby's room.

At almost seven months pregnant, Dani was starting to feel large. Her baby bump was now a perch large enough for her to rest her hands on. "How about we stick to off-white for now? I can add touches of color after the baby is born. With stuffed animals and pictures and things."

"Brilliant. I like that idea."

Dani felt rather proud. When shopping with Miriam, it wasn't often that she came up with the right answer. She called for a sales clerk to assist, and soon had an order for a rocking chair with a cream slip cover, and a beautiful sleigh-bed style crib. Next she and Miriam selected bedding for the crib, a circular rug for the floor and a change table.

"That's enough for one day." Dani felt decidedly poorer after leaving the store.

"Oh, no. Baby clothes, next," Miriam insisted. "But we can stop for some lunch if you want a rest."

They ate at an outside patio, where they could enjoy the warmth of the summer sun, while the ocean breeze kept them from getting too hot. Dani had a Cobb salad and a decaffeinated iced latte.

Miriam ordered the same salad, in a half-sized portion, and a regular iced latte. When the food arrived, however, she simply picked at it.

Dani wondered if she was worried about something. "Have your parents given up trying to convince you to move back to Vancouver?"

"I wish."

"Well, you're over twenty-one. They can't force you to move. Can they?"

"If I was making enough money to support myself, I'd agree with you. Unfortunately, I'm not." she shrugged.

"Tell me more about the work you do." All she knew was that Miriam designed book covers and edited manuscripts for authors who were self-publishing electronically. "What kind of clients do you have? Would I enjoy any of their books?"

Miriam gave a dramatic sigh. "I don't have clients. The truth is, I've been self-publishing my own books."

"You're an author yourself? That's amazing!"

"Not really. My books aren't selling very well. And most of the reviews I've had on Amazon have been terrible."

"Oh." It was hard to know what to say to that. "But, do you enjoy writing them? Because if you do—"

"I don't. Not really. They're hard core erotica. When I saw the money that woman who wrote *Shades Of Grey* was making, I figured, how hard can it be to write a book like that? Turns out it's plenty hard."

So like Miriam to look for the easy way. Marry a rich American. Write a bestselling book. Those were both ways to get a lot of money. But what was she really passionate about?

"Have you ever considered you might be writing in the wrong genre." Dani knew that what Miriam enjoyed reading were thriller and spy stories, with a bit of horror and paranormal thrown in.

"Probably. But—I'm scared to try something I really care about. Because, what if I'm not good at that, either?"

It was strange logic, but Dani understood it. Failing at something you didn't care about wasn't as awful as failing at something you did.

She thought of Adrian and their failed relationship. She hadn't seen him since that night they'd made love then broken up. Nor had she answered any of his text messages or emails. But she did read them and in the last one he'd told her he was taking Ava and the nanny for a month visit to Colorado to spend time with the grandparents. He hadn't asked how she was doing. In fact, she was pretty sure he didn't even know when her due date was.

She hadn't replied.

"Maybe you should try taking some writing courses," she suggested, trying to re-focus on Miriam. "And start work on a project that really interests you."

"I'll think about it." Miriam ate a few mouthfuls of her meal, and then set down her fork. "Don't tell Eliot about any of this okay? I'd hate for him to mock me about my awful books."

"I don't think he would. But of course I won't tell him,

if you don't want me to." But the request did get Dani thinking about the other night on the roof-top when Miriam had suggested marrying Eliot. When Eliot had reacted with shock, she'd immediately pretended it was a joke.

But maybe Miriam really did like him. Perhaps dating all those other guys had been just like her writing erotica stories. She'd been afraid to go after the man who really mattered.

∝ ∾

THE NEXT FRIDAY evening the three friends gathered at Eliot's place. Though she never would have admitted it out loud for fear of hurting Miriam's feelings, Dani loved getting together at Eliot's the best. For a man, he had a great ability to make a house feel like a home, and everything in his condo—the furniture, the pictures, even his collection of Native American sculpture—reflected some facet of his personality.

Plus, he had an amazing CD collection.

Dani squirreled into her favorite corner of the sectional as he whipped together his latest virgin cocktail creation while Miriam transferred the appetizers she'd picked up at Pike's Market onto a special blue plate that Eliot had pulled out and insisted she use.

For a straight guy, Eliot had great taste.

Assuming he was straight. Dani realized he hadn't mentioned any new girlfriends for some time now. When he handed her a peachy-colored drink in a fancy glass garnished with a slice of apricot, she popped the fruit into her mouth then decided to try the direct approach. "So, what's new with you?"

He seemed surprised that she'd asked. "You mean besides breaking up families and skimming off my share of the communal property?"

"You make your job sound so appealing. Have you ever thought of career counselling?"

"No. But I might just go into marriage counselling one day."

"That sounds interesting." Miriam set the tray of artfully arranged tapas on the cocktail table. "I take it you're trying to talk more of your clients into staying married?"

"I wish I could tell you the whole story. Unfortunately that wouldn't be ethical."

"Ethics are so boring." Miriam rolled her eyes as she sat.

"Tell me about it," he agreed, taking a spot between them.

"So if you can't talk to us about your work, let's talk about your love life." Dani nudged him with her toe. "You don't seem to be taking as many personal phone calls these days. Dry spell?"

"I haven't had a date in—months," he said, looking more surprised than anyone. "I must be losing my touch."

"Or maybe you're saving yourself for our Green Card Wedding." Miriam raised her eyebrows suggestively.

Eliot gave her a look that suggested not in a million years. He was so clearly not interested, that Dani felt a little sorry for Miriam.

"I suggest you try reconciling yourself to being Canadian. Lots of people would love to live in Canada," Eliot said reasonably.

"But it's so cold."

"I don't think the climate in Vancouver is much different from Seattle."

"But—I love my condo. And Pike's Market. And you guys don't live in Vancouver."

"He's just being a tease." Dani had been listening to the exchange quite certain that some of it was in jest, but not all. "Of course you can't move to Canada. We'd miss you too much. Maybe you could marry Mr. Bowman."

There was silence for two seconds and then Eliot burst out laughing, followed shortly by Miriam. Soon, all three of them were wiping tears from their eyes.

After that, they played a marathon of Kings Cribbage. Eliot was on a winning streak and eventually, Miriam and Dani had to concede and name him victor. They settled back into the soft pillows of the sectional sofa, while Eliot made them chai tea and pulled out a package of apricot and cardamom biscotti.

"You spoil us," Miriam said, accepting a mug with one of the biscotti arranged artfully on the side of the saucer.

Dani agreed. It was one of the reasons she loved coming to Eliot's best. Neither she nor Miriam ever served dessert on their nights to host. Hopefully she could stay awake long enough to enjoy hers. She couldn't stop yawning and her eyes were beginning to burn.

After he sat down to join them, Eliot noticed. "You're exhausted."

"No," she said, out of politeness, but she'd barely spoken

the word when another yawn overcame her. "Sorry. I'm such a party pooper."

"Hey. You've got a good excuse."

She'd put her feet up on the sectional and he reached over to squeeze one of her feet. It was a simple gesture— something a brother or a friend might do without thinking. But Dani felt a zap of something sexual between them. Here then gone so fast she wondered if she'd imagined it.

"So what are you doing for the rest of the weekend?" Eliot asked.

"I'm expecting a delivery from Pottery Barn tomorrow morning, so I'll be setting up the baby's room. I had the painters in last week so the room is ready." She laughed as her baby suddenly started moving. "I think Junior's pretty excited about it, too."

"Can I feel?" Miriam asked cautiously.

"Sure." Up until now Miriam had seemed almost grossed out whenever she'd invited her to feel the baby moving.

"Me, too?"

"Of course," she told Eliot. But when he placed his hand on her belly, she felt the sensation again and knew she hadn't imagined it earlier. She was, for some unknown reason, developing an attraction to one of her best friends. Pretty odd for a woman who was seven months pregnant with another man's child.

❧ ❦

THE NEXT MORNING Eliot waited until the Pottery Barn deliverymen had left Dani's before heading over himself. She opened the door dressed in her pregnancy jeans and a pretty pink blouse, and dirt encrusted gardening gloves.

"I'm here to make sure you don't do any heavy lifting," he said.

"No need. They assembled the crib and change table."

"Right. And you told them where to put them. And now that the men are gone you're wondering if the crib wouldn't look better against the other wall."

"You think you're so smart. The frustrating thing is that you're right." She laughed and opened the door wider.

The first thing he noticed was the sliding doors to her balcony were open. She followed his gaze.

"I was repotting the English ivy when they got here."

"Ah. That explains the dirty gloves. I was beginning to question your fashion judgment."

She wrinkled her nose at him. "I really think the ivy is much happier. Want to see?"

He didn't care too much about plants—not even the ivy which had been a gift from a happy client, Eliot had neglected to the point of near-death.

To make her happy, though, he went to see the ivy. The plant did look rather green and happy sitting in its new terra cotta pot, which didn't seem all that much bigger than its old one. When he pointed out this out to Dani she explained that the plant would go into shock if she transplanted it into a pot much bigger than the old one.

"I never knew that."

She shrugged. "Mom loved to garden. I'll probably never put to use half the things she taught me. But I know enough to doctor a few sickly houseplants back to life. Look at this orchid. I finally coaxed it into blooming again."

He duly admired the orchid, amused, and yes a little bit charmed, by how much time and attention Dani was willing to bestow on her motley collection of abandoned and forsaken plants. Her reputation had grown to the point that almost everyone in the building had brought her one of their plants at one time or another. Dani always returned them, along with a card of instructions on how to care for the plant, once they had recovered.

"So. The baby room?"

"Right." She pulled off the gardening gloves she'd been wearing and set them out on the balcony before leading him to the nursery.

The room kind of took him aback. He'd been expecting pastels. Building blocks and rainbows. That sort of thing.

But the room had been painted in calm neutrals. There was an arched alcove in the far wall where a mural of a tree had been painted. Into this place was nestled the crib. An elegant piece of furniture, stained a dark mahogany.

"Actually, the crib is perfect where it is."

"Yes. That wasn't what I wanted to move. I'd like to try switching around the change table and the rocking chair. So the chair is next to the window."

He saw what she meant and after insisting she not lift a thing herself, set about to try the new arrangement. When he was done they both realized that the original placement had been better. Without a word of complaint, he moved everything back to the way it had been.

"I'm so sorry."

"Hey, not a problem. I thought it would be better too."

He stood back again, taking in the room. An empty picture frame sitting on the upright chest of drawers, caught his attention. He lifted it up. "Hard to believe there's going to be a picture of a baby in this frame in, what? Less than two months."

"Crazy, isn't it?" She went to the crib, laid a hand on the bare mattress, as if trying to imagine her baby sleeping there. "Getting the room ready is really making this whole thing feel real."

She joined him at the bureau and opened one of the drawers. Inside were piles of tiny little undershirts, with bottoms attached. "Look at these onesies. Aren't they adorable?"

"So unbelievably small." He switched his gaze to her. Saw the awe and wonder in her eyes. "And beautiful, too."

Eliot wasn't a guy to play the "what if" game. But he did it then. *What if Dani was my woman, and she was carrying my child?* The idea didn't freak him out. It made him feel warm and happy inside.

Jeez. He had to get out of this room. "I was planning to go on a run this afternoon." She'd stopped joining him about three weeks ago. Now that she was getting larger, she preferred to walk. But he missed those times alone with her. "Want to catch a movie later?"

"Thanks but I'm planning to go to bed early. I have a long day planned at the lab and at five I'm going to my first prenatal class."

"What's that?"

"Oh, they're supposed to prepare new parents for the birthing process. According to my sister Mattie, there's nothing that really prepares a woman. Then again, she had twins."

He noticed the worry lines on her forehead. "The classes can't hurt, I'd guess."

"No."

She still didn't sound that keen about going. And then something occurred to him. "Do most women take their significant others with them?"

She nodded. "If not their husband or boyfriend, then a sister or a friend. I asked Miriam but she wasn't shy about saying no."

Miriam was an interesting woman. Funny and clever, sometimes kind, but not often very warm. The fact that she'd said no to Dani made him like her a little less.

"I'll go with you," he offered.

"What?"

She seemed almost shocked by the idea. Which was a little insulting.

"I'd like to think I'm as much your friend as Miriam is."

"Yes. But, Eliot. The classes are only part of the commitment—you would have to be with me for the birth of the baby."

"Oh." Now he was the one to be shocked. But it didn't take him long to wrap his mind around the idea. Since she was being firm about not telling her sisters until the baby was born, what other choice did she have?

"I could do it, Dani. You shouldn't have to go through something like that on your own."

"Since I'm going to be a single mother, I'd better get used to it."

August

ELIOT COULDN'T WAIT to get out of his office. He'd finished his last appointment, caught up with his e-mail and had left his phone programed with his standard—"I'm out of the office, my assistant Paige Blythe will be happy to help you"—message.

God bless Paige. She'd been especially wonderful today, buzzing in and out of his office. "You need to sign this before you go, and return these calls. No, leave that memo. I can take care of that tomorrow—"

He took a final look at his clean desk top. Generally he managed to clear the deck just two times a year: before Christmas break and before his summer vacation. Some lawyers he knew liked to be this organized every day. But he would never be that guy.

Before leaving he stopped in to say a few goodbyes, ending with Paige. "Well, I'm off. You know the drill—only phone me if it's something urgent."

She nodded, her ponytail still tidy even now at the end of the day. "Have a great holiday."

"I intend to." He tapped her desk. "Good luck. See you in two weeks."

Humming the old rock standard, *School's out for the*

summer, he headed for the elevator. Within seconds he was going to be free—

"Eliot! Hang on. A call just came in."

It was Paige. Damn it. He'd been so close. Reluctantly he turned around. "Is it—?"

"Lizbeth Greenway just had her baby. And her husband wants to speak with you."

The news caught him off guard. Made him think of Dani and the fact that in just five weeks, he could be getting a call like this about her. He shook off the reverie and went to take the phone from Paige. "Eliot here."

"It's a boy," was the first thing Nick Greenway blurted. "Liz had a boy."

Not *we.* But *Liz.* "That's great!"

"Is it?"

Eliot could hear the anguish behind Nick's question. Gently he responded with a few questions of his own. "Is the baby healthy? Is Lizbeth okay?"

"Yeah. The baby's good. Liz came through alright, too. It was tough, but so was she."

"Well, then. It is great, right?"

"I guess. I don't know."

Eliot sighed, frustrated suddenly at himself. He should have simply filed the divorce papers the way Lizbeth Greenwood had asked him to do in the first place. Why had he thought he could help this couple?

"Look, Nick. If you want to sort out your feelings, you should call a therapist. If you want legal counsel about leaving your wife, you should get yourself your own lawyer.

But if you want my advice as a man, Lizbeth is still your wife and she's just been through a pretty major ordeal. Focus on what she needs for the next few days. And worry about yourself later."

There was a stunned silence, then Nick mumbled a few words and hung up.

Eliot went to hand the phone to Paige, but she was clapping.

"Well said, boss."

Eliot blinked. Then smiled. "You think?"

"Oh, I do. All the time. Now get going on that holiday. You deserve it."

☙ ❧

DANI PULLED OUT her suitcase to pack for her holiday. The past four weeks had been stressful and she needed the break.

Fortunately, she could leave with a clear conscience, since just last night she'd completed her prenatal sessions. The classes had been interesting, and helpful to some extent. But she'd felt like such an odd-man-out being the only expectant mother without a partner.

A few times she regretted turning down Eliot's offer. But when she thought about the unexpected sexual jolts she'd begun experiencing in his company, the way she'd started to notice and appreciate his lean, muscular body—she knew she'd been right to turn him down. Hormonal fluctuations from her pregnancy had to be causing this new attraction toward a man she'd always considered just a friend.

But she certainly didn't want to put herself to the test by

having him give her back rubs, and coach her breathing.

No, she was going to be fine giving birth on her own. And she wouldn't be alone, of course. There would be nurses. And her doctor. By now she'd had so many appointments, Gwen Fong seemed more like a trusted friend than her OB.

What did have Dani a little anxious was the prospect of spending two weeks at the cottage with Eliot. Was it a smart plan given these unexpected new feelings of hers? But Miriam would be with them. So, it would be fine. And anyway, every day she was growing larger, more awkward and uncomfortable. Surely soon, she'd be beyond any sort of sexual reaction, at all.

From a work perspective, Dani was satisfied, too. She'd put in long days at the lab all July knowing she wouldn't be coming back until after the baby was born. She'd completed the long to-do list Jenna had given her, updating all her files, backing them up and filing a copy with Jenna for good measure.

Dani could tell her boss wasn't sure she'd be coming back after the baby was born. She wished she could reassure Jenna somehow. Yes, she was about to become a mother. But she also loved this job. Furthermore, she believed the research they were doing was going to help parents raise healthy, successful, well-adjusted children in the future. Who wouldn't be motivated to go to work every morning with a goal like that?

Out of a desire to leave her office in perfect order, and to reassure Jenna about her commitment to their work, Dani stayed late every night before her holiday. Her body was exacting a price for the long hours. Back aches and swollen feet being two of the most annoying. But she didn't mind putting in the effort, knowing her reward would be two glorious weeks of relaxing at the cottage, reading and sleeping as much as she liked—with the occasional game of Kings Cribbage or Scrabble thrown in.

What lay beyond the holiday—a few weeks of final preparations, then the birth of her baby—Dani couldn't really imagine. Her life was going to be so different, but how it would feel, and what it would be like, she had no idea.

Including whether Adrian would play any role at all in their child's life.

She hadn't heard from him since he'd left on holiday with Ava. As far as she knew he was still visiting family. Didn't it occur to him that her due date must be approaching?

Not that she expected him to come to the hospital with her and hold her hand. But, yes, Dani finally admitted to herself the night before her holiday as she was packing her suitcase, she had nursed a tiny hope that he might want to be there with her.

With her open suitcase on her bed, Dani perused her clothing choices. She didn't have much to pick from. Hardly anything fit. She wasn't sure she had the nerve to wear a bikini now that she was eight months pregnant. But she'd seen models on the covers of magazines doing it, and since she hadn't bought a maternity bathing suit, she added the least skimpy of her bikinis to the small pile of T-shirts and sundresses she'd already selected. For the cool evenings she had a hoodie and a windbreaker, both of which fit only if she didn't zip them up.

Next she added her travel toiletry bag. For sleeping she packed the humungous T-shirt she'd bought at the Copper Mountain Rodeo last fall—never guessing at the time that within the year she'd fill every inch of the voluminous garment.

Done.

She closed the suitcase and set it next to the book bag crammed with her reading material for the holidays. A motley collection of professional journals and beach reads, with a few literary classics thrown in for good measure. She'd always meant to read *Crossing to Safety* by Wallace Stegner. Maybe this year she'd actually do it.

Tenderly, she ministered to her plants, hoping Mr. Boswell wouldn't overwater them when he came in to check on them next week.

Finally, it was time to sleep. Eliot had warned them he wanted to make an early start the next day. Dani crawled under the covers, taking her phone with her. She stared at the notifications, wishing one would pop up from Adrian.

Of course, she could be the one to reach out. Give him a call or send him a message. But what if he gave her the cold shoulder? Worse, mentioned something about his lawyer again.

No. She'd be smarter to wait. Let him make the next move.

She was setting her alarm for the next morning when a

text message popped on the screen.

"All packed?"

She felt a leveling of emotions when she saw it was only Eliot. "You bet."

"See you at eight. We'll stop for coffee and muffins on the road."

Dani smiled. Despite her worries about the future, even despite missing Adrian, she was looking forward to this trip.

❦ ❦

"GOD, MIRIAM. WE'RE just going to the beach. How can you possibly need this much stuff?" Despite the complaint, Eliot tossed both of her vintage-inspired, Kate Spade suitcases into the back of his SUV, along with Dani's utilitarian black bag and his own leather duffel.

"Careful! You're worse than the airline baggage handlers." Miriam used a tissue to wipe a smudge from the side of one of the cases.

Dani had to admit the luggage set—which she'd watched Miriam order on-line—was a thing of beauty. The bags were white with brown leather detailing and bright yellow handles. No less a thing of beauty was Miriam herself, in a black and white striped mini-dress that fit her petite figure like a second skin. Her dark hair was pulled back with a gold hair clip and her Tom Ford sunglasses made her look like a movie star.

Next to her friend, Dani felt like a cow. "I'll sit in the back."

"You'll have more room in the front," Eliot said. He also

looked fashionable, yet masculine, in a pair of plaid shorts, light green golf shirt and dock shoes. His six-foot-two inch body, tanned and muscular, didn't hurt.

"I'll be fine," Dani insisted, climbing up to the seat and trying to make herself comfortable without flopping around like a seal.

As promised, Eliot stopped at a coffee shop before they left the city where they picked up breakfast and coffees to go. Back in the SUV, Dani tried not to complain about her decaf latte. But it was difficult when she could smell the real stuff. She leaned forward and inhaled deeply.

"I miss drinking real coffee more than I miss wine."

"Bet you reverse that statement around five this afternoon," Eliot challenged.

Dani groaned. Happy hour on the beach was definitely not going to be the same this year.

"I don't know where you get your willpower," Miriam said. "And is it really necessary? Surely a few cups of coffee or glasses of wine won't hurt the baby. As long as you don't go crazy."

"Actually studies have shown that even a small amount of caffeine carries the risk of fetal growth restriction."

"You sound like such a professor sometimes, Dani."

"How odd," Eliot said drily, his gaze in the rear-view mirror meeting Dani's.

"Smaller babies," Dani amended, translating the lingo for Miriam.

"Isn't that be a good thing? I mean, you've got to deliver this thing, right?" She looked over her shoulder at Dani, pushing her sunglasses higher on the bridge of her nose at the same time. "Won't it come out easier if it's smaller?"

Dani tried not to resent the way she referred to the baby as '*it*'. "Yes. But in general smaller babies are less healthy babies and carry greater risk of miscarriage or being still-born." Without conscious intent, Dani's hands had gone protectively to her belly. Her secret fear nibbled at her consciousness, so much so that she almost said something. *And I don't want to add to my baby's risk factors when already there's a chance something will be wrong—*

But Miriam was talking again, and the moment was lost.

"Seeing everything you've been through has convinced me that I never want to have kids," Miriam said.

"What if your Green Card husband wants a family?" Eliot teased.

"Hmm. Well, maybe. But he'd have to be really sweet to me."

This comment, a reminder that Dani was in this pregnancy alone, without a partner to be sweet to her, also stung, though Dani knew Miriam hadn't meant it to. She sighed, then settled back into her seat and took a sip of the insipid decaffeinated latte. For the next while she let her thoughts drift as Miriam engaged Eliot in a conversation that was difficult for her to hear, and therefore impossible for her to contribute to.

She felt her spirits begin to lift as they left the city behind and vistas of the Pacific peeked out from beyond the highways, offices and condo complexes of Seattle. Having grown up in land-locked Montana, the ocean still seemed exotic to Dani. No matter how long she lived here, she suspected she would always feel this way.

The vast and powerful Pacific Ocean nurtured creatures so different from the deer, elk, cattle, horses, dogs and cats she'd been surrounded by all her life. Last summer she and Eliot had seen dolphins and humpback whales when they were out on the kayak. Sea lions were a common sight and otters often came right up on the dock when they were in a playful mood.

When the tide was out they dug clams and picked oysters right on the beach. Other times Dani would pick out interesting seashells and sand dollars for the glass jar collections in the cottage. Patrolling the air were pelicans, cormorants and albatrosses, as well as the great blue heron and, of course, the bald eagle.

All of this seaside magic came back to her as the miles flew by.

They stopped in Belfair for groceries, then pushed through to the seaside cottage which Eliot's grandparents had purchased over sixty years ago. The two-story, timber-frame home was rarely used since his mother's death, especially as family members had moved to follow careers and opportunities in other parts of the country. But a property management firm kept the place well-maintained and clean and when Eliot unlocked the front door, they were greeted with the fresh scent of lavender wafting from a generous bouquet on the kitchen island.

The walls and vaulted ceiling were finished in larch and the floors were smooth slate in the entry way and though to the kitchen. Dani dropped the two grocery bags she'd been carrying to the island, then rushed off to the bathroom while Miriam supervised Eliot putting away the stores.

When Dani returned to the kitchen five minutes later she felt much more comfortable. "Sorry I ran off like that. My bladder's gone from vente-sized, to grande, to small in the past eight months."

"Why didn't you say so in Belfair? We could have stopped at a place with restrooms." Eliot was crouched in front of the wine fridge, unpacking the bottles Miriam had added to their grocery cart. She'd selected some expensive vintages, but had said nothing when it came time to pay the tab, letting Dani be the one to cover the bill over Eliot's protests.

Dani didn't know if Miriam truly was more annoying these days, or if Dani's pregnancy was making her less tolerant. In any case, it would be a long two weeks if things kept on this way. She handed over a bag of tinned goods. "Put these away would you? As I recall they go in the corner pantry."

Miriam said nothing, just took the bag and dutifully did as requested, while Dani stocked the fridge with their vegetables, cheese and meat. Once all the food was taken care of, Eliot carried their suitcases to the bedrooms. Dani was pleased to be given the same corner-room she'd occupied last year. It was smaller than Miriam's but the attached bathroom had an old-fashioned, claw-footed tub that molded perfectly to her back. She was looking forward to a long soak tonight.

"What do you want to do first?" Eliot asked them, standing in the hall outside his room. He always left his parents' master room vacant, taking instead the room he'd used as a boy. "Unpack? Go for a walk on the beach?"

"How about we sit on the deck and open a bottle of that nice bubbly?" Miriam suggested. "Toast the first day of our holiday."

She was looking at Eliot as she said this, and not for the first time, Dani felt like the third wheel. Again her annoyance flared, but was it fair? It wasn't Miriam's fault that Dani couldn't drink. Maybe what she was really resenting, wasn't the things Miriam was saying—because it was totally in character for her to suggest opening a bottle of champagne like this—but the fact that Miriam looked so damn pretty and adorable while she felt like a big, fat loser.

"You two go ahead. I'm actually wiped. I think I need a nap."

Eliot had looked disposed to veto Miriam's suggestion until Dani mentioned needing a nap. "Sure, Dani. Whatever you like. If you feel like a walk when you wake up, let me know."

"Have a good rest," Miriam added, already on her way down the stairs. "You look like you need it."

An urge to take a couple of books and hurl them down the stairs suddenly swept over Dani. But just as quickly the anger left her. She *was* tired. She hadn't been making it up as some sort of excuse to get out of drinking wine with her friends.

Sighing, she slipped into her corner bedroom.

The iron bed stand was painted white, except for the

corner brass bedposts. A beautiful sea-blue quilt was spread over the queen-sized mattress, and a sprig of lavender had been placed on the folded-over edge of the white cotton sheet beneath.

Dani picked up the lavender and inhaled deeply. Such a lovely scent. Her mother had grown lavender in her herb garden behind the house at the Circle C. Dani remembered how the bees had loved it, buzzing drunkenly over the deep purple flowers on the hot summer days of early July.

After washing up, Dani changed into her sleeping T-shirt, then opened all three of the windows in her room. Soon a salty sea breeze was freshening the air, and she pulled back the covers to the bed looking more forward to her nap than she'd expected.

Her eyes were just closing when she heard the three-note tone from her phone signaling a message from Adrian.

Suddenly alert, she pulled her phone from her purse so she could read the message.

"We just got back to Seattle. Any chance I can see you tonight?"

❧ ❦

DANI AWOKE TO the sounds of seagulls and crashing waves. And voices, disjointed bits of conversation.

She rolled over, brushed the hair out of her eyes and listened.

"—not the same—"

A female voice. Probably Miriam.

"I'm just saying," the same voice continued.

A deeper rumble followed, Dani assumed it was Eliot. But this time she couldn't make out any of the words.

She eased her way out of the lavender-scented sheets, then pulled off her T-shirt. God, her stomach was huge. She smoothed her hands over it, imagining the baby inside. "You okay in there?"

Dani had been tested enough in her life to know that her IQ fell in the top one percent of the population. She suspected Adrian's was at least that high. With those kind of genes, her baby had to be smart, right? Even if she wasn't as smart as her parents, that would be fine. As long as she could live a normal life.

Eliot had left her suitcase on a bench so Dani didn't even need to bend over far to open it. Quickly, she unpacked her meagre clothing into an empty bureau drawer and hung her dresses in the closet. One of them, a pretty white cotton eyelet shift, she decided to slip on now, along with a pair of flip flops.

She brushed her hair, put on a hat, then went to join her friends on the back deck, stopping first to get a bottle of iced tea from the fridge.

The first thing she saw was Miriam on a lounge chair, wearing a cinnamon-red bikini. Eliot, in swimming trunks, was relaxing in the chair next to her. The bottle of bubbly was empty and they were both drinking from clear plastic water glasses that Dani doubted contained water.

"Here you are!"

Unless he was pretending, Eliot looked happy to see her. Miriam, less so. She gave Dani's outfit a derisive once-over.

"You should have let me take you shopping for some beach clothes last week when I offered."

"I can't get motivated to buy clothes I'm only going to wear another month. I have enough to get by." She smoothed her hands over the shift. "This is comfortable and cool."

"Perfect for the cottage," Eliot declared. He set down his glass and eased up from the cushioned lounge chair. "Ready for that walk?"

Dani nodded. She could sip her drink at the same time. Right now she needed to get her circulatory system in gear. She glanced at Miriam to see if she would join them, but the other woman was already absorbed in the fashion magazine that had been face-down beside her on the chair just half a minute earlier.

A series of wooden stairs led down about fifteen feet to the beach. The cottage had been built on the point of a bay, where at least five hundred yards separated them from the next property owners. She and Eliot automatically fell into step beside one another.

"How was the bubbly?"

He shrugged. "I only drank two glasses of the stuff to prevent Miriam from downing the entire bottle herself. I don't know what's gotten into her lately. Does she seem— edgy to you?"

Edgy was the perfect word to describe the change in Miriam. "I feel like she's mad at me for getting pregnant. For changing the dynamic of our group."

Eliot gave her a long, unreadable look. "Maybe that's it."

The humidity of the sea air had brought out the curl in his hair. The effect was quite charming, giving him a slightly roguish appearance that wasn't hurt at all by his broad muscular shoulders, well developed pecs, and ridged ab muscles. Had he been this well-toned last year, too?

She kind of thought he had. Yet somehow, last year, his build hadn't really registered with her.

But she had to stop thinking of Eliot this way. He'd no doubt laugh at her right now if he could read her mind.

She took a sip of her iced tea, then looked out at the ocean view again. "I can't believe your brothers don't visit more often. This is so beautiful."

"They have busy lives. Demanding careers. And the cottage isn't exactly easy to get to."

"What are they like? Are the three of you quite similar?"

"Hard for me to say. You'll meet them one day. Then you can decide for yourself."

"You think I will? Meet them?" She remembered one of them coming to town shortly after she'd met Eliot. As far as she could recall he hadn't had another family visit since then. They never even got together for Thanksgiving or Christmas.

"Yes. At least I hope so." Eliot looked like he wanted to say something else, but then her phone gave out a familiar three-note chime.

She couldn't resist pulling the phone from her pocket to check the message. Before going to sleep she'd sent Adrian a reply saying she was at Eliot's cottage on Hood Canal and couldn't see him for a while.

He'd responded: "For how long?"

Dani tucked the phone away.

"Adrian?" Eliot guessed.

She hesitated, then nodded. "After four weeks of silence, he suddenly wants to see me."

"The guy has seriously bad timing."

"Yeah." She tried to smile.

"You want to go back?"

"No. God, no," she answered quickly and she could tell Eliot was relieved. The problem was, however, part of her *did* want to pack her bag and hurry back to see Adrian.

How pathetic was that?

❧ ❦

AFTER THEIR WALK, Dani took a book to one of the comfy chairs at the front porch and settled in for a couple hours of reading. Eliot had offered to cook dinner that evening and was prepping food in the kitchen. Despite his assurances that he didn't need any help, Miriam was in there with him.

Probably working on her second bottle of wine.

Dani wrinkled her nose at herself, for having such an uncharitable thought. So what if Miriam was kicking up her heels a little. This was a holiday after all, and last year Dani hadn't been shy about drinking her own share of alcohol, as well. In fact, she remembered one afternoon when they'd gone through three pitchers of sangria with little problem.

When she finished Chapter Six, Dani decided she'd had enough of the story for now and set the book aside. Fatalistically she pulled out her phone and re-read the stream of text messages she and Adrian had exchanged in the past two hours.

"Back in two weeks," she'd said, in response to his question.

"Call me as soon as you're back."

"I will. Everything OK?"

"Fine. Just need to talk. You OK?"

"Yes."

"Good. Take care. See you in 2 wks."

She kept trying to read in more than was really there. Like, had he changed his mind about her and the baby? It had to be a good sign that he'd asked how she was doing. However, he hadn't done so until she'd asked about him. So.

Dani longed to ask Miriam her opinion. A few months ago she would have. But their friendship had changed and Dani no longer trusted her the way she once had. Which left Eliot, but she didn't need to ask to know what he would say.

He'd tell her Adrian was a jerk and she was better off without him.

Easy advice to give if you were a guy.

✌ ✍

THEY ATE DINNER on the back deck. Grilled salmon and veggies with pesto linguine. Another bottle of wine opened by Miriam, while Dani stuck to her unsweetened iced teas.

Before dinner Miriam had showered and changed into her third outfit of the day, this one a short, midnight blue halter dress with a deep v neck-line and no back to speak of. The fabric was thin enough that the peaks of her nipples were hard to ignore.

God, to have such cute, perky breasts. Her sister Callan had breasts like that. Not Dani though. Hers had been full B cups even before she was pregnant. Who knew what they'd be like after?

But when she thought about nursing her baby, about holding her tiny daughter or son in her arms and feeling him or her warm against her skin, she didn't care. Not really.

After dinner the three of them sat and talked while they watched the sunset. For a while it was like old times. Eliot pulled out the cottage Scrabble set—an earlier version than they usually played with, tiles smooth with use, the board bearing rings from coffee mugs and a few red wine spills as well.

Dani won the first game, Eliot the second. The three of them were usually well-matched, but in both games Miriam's score was markedly the lowest.

"I'm drawing lousy letters tonight. No wonder I keep losing."

Dani glanced at Eliot, who raised his eyebrows at her. It hadn't been the letters. Miriam's drinking was the reason she hadn't won a game, or even made a decent score.

But neither she nor Eliot said anything as Miriam got up from the table, not bothering to help put the letters back into the red velvet bag. After topping up her wine glass, she went to sit on the chair next to Eliot. "Tell me the truth. Do you think I'm pretty?"

She was leaning in toward him as she said this, pressing her chest into his arm.

"It's not like you to have an inferiority complex." Eliot shifted back in his chair, increasing the space between them. "You know you're attractive."

"Well sure. But I've always wondered, what sort of woman turns you on, Eliot? You've dated so many different types over the years. I still don't have a handle on what you like."

"If I have a type, it isn't based on hair color or body shape, if that's what you mean."

Dani could tell he was started to get annoyed. But Miriam was too far gone to take the hint and back off.

"So, you can't even say if you prefer, oh—" Her gaze drifted toward Dani—"tall, full-figured women over petite, slender ones?"

"What the hell? Miriam, you've had too much to drink."

"But maybe you're just not into Asians. Is that the problem?"

"Stop it. Seriously." Eliot got out of his chair, took the bottle of wine and forced the cork back into the neck. "I think it's time we wrapped up this party for the night."

"I agree totally." Dani had been wondering how to extradite herself from this suddenly uncomfortable situation. "I'll put away the Scrabble Game. See you guys in the morning."

"Wait, I'll—"

She heard Eliot call after her, and felt a little guilty about leaving him alone with Miriam while she was in this strange mood of hers. But she'd had enough drama for one day. Tomorrow, she hoped, everyone would be back to normal.

❧ ❧

"WHAT'S COME OVER you tonight?" Until now, Eliot had never experienced a woman acting like a "clinging vine." But as he plucked Miriam's hands off his shoulders, that was exactly the metaphor he was reminded of.

"Nothing's *come over me* as you put it. I'm just tired of the games."

"What? You mean Scrabble?" Why hadn't she said something earlier? They could have played something else.

"No, you fool. The games between you and me."

"Hang on." She was coming at him again, putting her hand on his arm. "There is no game going on with you and me."

"Then why won't you be upfront with me?" She leaned in, practically shoving her boobs into his face. "Are you attracted, or not?"

He took hold of her shoulders and held her at arm's length. "If you're asking me to be your Green Card man again, I'm sorry. I won't do it."

Her laugh had a bitter, almost desperate quality that chilled him.

"I don't want a Green Card marriage. I never have."

"What the hell?" For as long as he'd known her it was almost all she talked about.

"I want you, Eliot. That's all. Just you."

Holy crap. His head was spinning now, even though she'd been the one to drink all that wine. He tried to think if he'd led her on. If so, it had been accidental. Shit. What a mess. Why had Dani skipped off to bed so quickly?

"Look, I'm sorry. I never meant to give you the idea that I was interested in being anything but friends."

"Seriously?" Miriam twisted away from his touch. She raised her chin and scanned her hands over her body. "You're going to turn down this body? Do you have any idea how many other guys want to date me? I had my profile up online for just twenty-four hours and I had—"

"Stop. I know you're beautiful Miriam. You don't have to prove it to me."

"Then, why don't you want me?"

"It's not that simple."

"Some people would say that it is. Exactly that simple. You're attracted to me and I'm attracted to you."

But he hadn't said he was attracted to her. He'd said she was beautiful. And there was a difference.

"Miriam, I don't know what to say. We've been friends for a long time. But being together that way—it's not going to happen. It just isn't."

She balled her hands into fists and glared at him. He could feel the anger radiating off of her.

"It's *Dani,* isn't it?" she spewed out with acidic bitterness.

"What the hell?"

"You love Dani. You always have. I didn't want to see it. But it's been pretty obvious, right from the start."

"That's crazy!"

"I couldn't agree more. She's pregnant with another man's child. *Another man's child.* And you still prefer her to me."

"I'm not dignifying that with an answer."

"Why? Afraid of *perjuring* yourself?"

In that moment Eliot hated Miriam. She was pushy. Obnoxious. And she'd finally gone way too far.

"I'm going for a run." He had to get away from her before he said or did something he'd regret. He kicked off his sandals, raced down the stairs to the beach, and began jogging along the sandy shore, no, not jogging, running. He widened his stance and pumped his arms. Just enough light was coming from the waxing moon that he was able to keep from stumbling into driftwood or wandering off track. For five minutes he gave the run all he had, and then slowed to a true jog, and finally a walk.

The hell of it was, Miriam was partly right. He did have a bit of a soft spot for Dani. Not because she was beautiful—which she was. Or because she was so bright and interesting—which she also was. But because of her soft, tender side. Before she'd become pregnant he'd only glimpsed it occasionally. But when he did, man, it took him down. It made his own heart go soft and mushy, too.

Since the pregnancy, he'd seen even more of that quality in her. And so, yes, he was becoming more drawn to her in a way.

But love?

No. He knew how she felt about Adrian. Even though that jerk didn't deserve her, she was still totally into him. Just a text message from the guy tied her in knots.

So no, he didn't love her the way Miriam thought he

did. He just cared. In a way he could never picture himself caring about Miriam, because Miriam didn't often spare a thought for anyone but herself.

❧ ❦

DANI HAD A restless sleep. Odd dreams. Her parents were arguing, then a door slammed and she heard a car drive off in the night. Waking briefly, she wondered what that had been about. She often dreamed about her mother, but hadn't had the old nightmares about her parents fighting for over a decade.

Eventually, she fell back asleep and the next time she awoke, the sun was shining in from the east-facing window and the house was very quiet. Suspecting she was the first one awake—and that Miriam would have one hell of a headache and be very grouchy if awoken—Dani quietly slipped on her clothes and made her way downstairs.

Someone had made coffee and recently, because it still smelled great. With a pang of self-pity, she put the kettle on to boil, then put an herbal tea bag into a mug. If she couldn't have coffee, she reasoned she at least deserved one of the coconut lemon muffins they'd bought at the grocery store yesterday. Adding a handful of the washed berries she found, still dripping wet in a colander in the sink, she took her breakfast to the back deck.

Given the pot of coffee, she wasn't surprised to see Eliot already sitting at one of the four chairs around the teak table. He was wearing swimming trunks, water droplets glistening on his skin and in his hair from the morning sun. He'd either just gotten out of the shower without toweling off, or had been in the ocean. She decided to go for the ocean.

"Good morning. How's the water?"

"Salty. Cold."

She took a closer look and noticed dark circles under reddened eyes. He hadn't shaved, which wasn't unusual since this was a holiday. But he sure didn't look like he was having much fun, despite the delicious fresh coffee he must have just consumed judging by his almost empty mug.

She settled in the chair opposite from him, where a strategically placed umbrella shielded her from direct sunlight. "Too much to drink last night? I thought it was just Miriam."

"It was Miriam all right." He slugged back the rest of his coffee. "God, I needed that. I'm going for more. Can I get you anything?"

"No. I'm fine." She frowned trying to figure out what was going on with him. Eliot wasn't a moody man. Something major had to be wrong. "Are you okay?"

He hesitated at the double French doors. "Sort of. By the way, Miriam's left."

"What?"

But he didn't stay to answer and she had to wait almost fifteen minutes before he returned with a tray containing his re-filled coffee cup and a stack of toast along with a jar of honey and another of peanut butter.

She waited until he'd lathered one of the slices first with the peanut butter, then the honey. She even let him take a few bites before she asked him again, "What did you just say, a few minutes ago? Something about Miriam leaving?"

"She's gone. She left last night. Around five, I think it was. She'd finished off a pot of coffee, so hopefully she was sober by then."

"But—why? And how?"

"She took my SUV."

"You let her take your SUV? But what are we going to use for a vehicle while we're here? And how will we get home?" She couldn't believe how calm he was acting. Preparing a second piece of toast as if all he had to worry about was eating his breakfast.

"I guess we'll have to arrange for a rental car. And I didn't let her have the SUV. She took the keys out of my shorts' pocket."

Dani could feel her eyes widen. "While you were wearing them?"

"No. She came into my room while I was sleeping. Or trying, at any rate."

"And she just took your keys? Without permission?"

"Yup."

"I—I can't believe this." Obviously there was a lot more to the story. She waited until he'd finished his second piece of toast. "So, are you going to fill me in?"

"This stupid Green Card wedding idea of hers. She started pushing it again. I finally told her outright there was no way in hell I was doing that for her. Well, she got pissed off. That's why she left."

"I don't think she was just after her Green Card. She has feelings for you."

He was quiet for a moment, then nodded. "Yeah. I know. I feel like a shit. But—" He shrugged, and she knew he was saying that he didn't feel that way about Miriam.

"Poor, Miriam. But it's not your fault. So try not to feel like a shit, okay?"

He managed a grin, but it didn't last long. "I'm going to call for a rental car when I'm done here. So what do you think? Do you want to head back to Seattle, too? Or stay for the duration?"

Dani took a moment to think. The entire dynamic of the holiday would change without Miriam. But given how hugely pregnant she was right now, she didn't think she needed to worry about being alone with Eliot. And she needed this break. Besides, if she went home now, Adrian would think she was rushing back because he wanted to see her. Not a good idea.

"I'd like to stay. If you do."

"Good. Yeah. I want to stay. I just wasn't sure how you'd feel. You know, without a chaperone and all."

She patted her belly. "I've got an onboard chaperone these days."

And so it was decided. Eliot arranged to have a rental car dropped off at the cottage so they'd be able to get into town when they needed groceries or when she had a craving for chocolate mint ice-cream. Something that seemed to happen on a regular basis.

Eliot kept active, swimming in the mornings, going for runs in the evening, but Dani was content to take a few shorter walks during the day. It didn't take much for her to lose her breath now, and she spent hours reading, and also compiling lists of baby names. Though, if she had a girl, there was really only one name that seemed right to her—her Mom's—Beverly.

Every afternoon around five, she and Eliot would have a game of Scrabble or cribbage, then prepare dinner together. In the evenings, they read, often sharing interesting snippets with one another.

They were like an old, married couple, and it was surprisingly nice. At times Dani felt certain Eliot must be bored to tears, but he really seemed quite content to pass their days quietly. Halfway through their holiday, they were sitting on the front porch reading when Dani became aware of Eliot watching her.

She immediately felt self-consciously aware of her uncombed hair and the tea stain at the bottom of her T-shirt. "What's the matter?"

"Excuse me if I'm being rude. But your stomach is twitching."

"The baby has hiccups."

"Seriously?"

"Yeah. Want to feel?" She placed his hand on her belly and watched his eyes go round with fascination.

"I had no idea that happened."

"Nine months ago, neither did I."

"I can't imagine what it must be like for you."

"It's pretty incredible," she admitted. There were a lot of things she actually loved about being pregnant. What she didn't love was watching her body turn into an ungainly blob while with every day of their holiday Eliot became more tanned, more fit, more absolutely gorgeous. And what was really crazy was how well the two of them got along when Miriam wasn't around.

One of the books Eliot had brought with him to the cottage was a memoir written by a former American Secretary of State. One evening they stayed up until past two, discussing various issues raised in the book and, as Eliot put it, solving all the problems in the world. Dani had never noticed before how similar their views were on matters of the environment and politics.

Five days into the holiday, Adrian sent her a text asking if there was any chance she would come home early.

Dani took a lot of satisfaction in answering, "Having a really good time. Will be back Aug 20 as planned." After she hit "send" she noticed Eliot watching.

"Adrian?"

"He was wondering if I would cut my holiday short."

"So, he wants to see you?"

"I guess." Eliot made no further comment. But she could tell he wasn't happy about the idea.

∂∞ ∞

EIGHT DAYS INTO the holiday the weather went from pleasant and mostly sunny to hot. Eliot's body was dry almost immediately after his morning swim. He came up from the beach to find Dani at the outdoor table, where a thermos of coffee and stack of toast was waiting for him.

"You shouldn't have gone to all this trouble."

"Toast and coffee isn't trouble. Your swim must have been nice. It's already so hot out." She lifted her hair off her neck, then fasted a band around it to make a ponytail. He hadn't seen her wear make-up once this trip, but she had the sort of creamy skin that didn't need it. A few freckles had popped up along the bridge of her nose.

Cute.

They took turns sharing bits of morning news from their iPads as they munched their way through the plate of toast. He noticed she ate hers with the sour cherry jam they'd purchased at the local Farmer's Market.

At quarter to ten, she shut down the iPad. "I'm done. It's too hot here, even under the umbrella. I'm going to take my book to the porch and read for a while."

"You could go for a swim to cool down." He hadn't seen her in a bathing suit yet, and had to admit he was curious.

"Maybe later."

Though he was making an effort to unplug from the office for the two weeks, Eliot decided to check in with Paige and see how things were going. He went into the house to make the call, planting himself in front of the windows overlooking the ocean. Hell of a view. He ought to get out here more often.

"Morning Eliot. How's the holiday going?"

He thought of the ugly first day, having to turn Miriam down when she'd come on to him on the beach. Then later, when she'd tried to slip naked into his bed, he'd had to physically push her away, at which point she'd stolen his keys and told him to go to hell.

"Rocky start, but it's good now. How are things there?"

She gave him a quick update on his files, sounding as organized as if she'd been expecting him to call. And probably she had, he realized.

"That sounds fine. I won't check in again until I'm back at work next Monday. Call me if something urgent comes up."

"Will do. Oh—I almost forgot. We did get a call from Lizbeth Greenway yesterday. She wants to proceed with her divorce."

He wasn't surprised, but he couldn't help also feeling a little sad. "Set her up in a meeting with Katherine or Gerald. Whoever has time. Did she mention how she's doing with the new baby?"

"They're both fine. She's still living with her sister. Or is it cousin? Apparently Nick has only seen the baby once."

"Well. That says everything, I guess."

"It was sweet of you to try to help them."

"Obviously I should stick to the law from now on."

Paige just laughed. She knew him too well.

Eliot went for another swim after that. He thought he knew why the Greenway case got to him so much. Every time he thought of Lizbeth, he couldn't help being reminded of Dani. She was being so brave about this whole pregnancy and single motherhood thing. But sometimes she had to be scared. He sure as hell would be.

Eliot dove into the water, then flipped over to float on his back. The buoyant ocean water soothed his over-heated skin and he stayed out for at least twenty minutes enjoying the moment, the blue of the sky above, his body moving with the gentle waves. When he flipped over to swim to shore, he noticed Dani on the deck, pulling her oversized T-shirt over her head.

Underneath she was wearing a tiny bikini that showed off her long-legged, pregnant body to perfection. As she started toward the water, he couldn't help noticing that the triangle patches of her top barely covered a third of her generous breasts. And her belly—the size of a basketball, he'd guess—sat nicely above the small swath of her bikini bottoms.

He stood up in water that hit him at the waist, thinking it would be good to keep the lower half of his body cool.

He'd never expected to get turned on by the sight of a pregnant woman in a bathing suit. But Dani—she looked fabulous.

"It got too hot, even on the porch," she explained as she began to wade into the water. "Oh, man, this feels good."

"That it does." He waited for her to reach him, then suggested they swim out to the buoy marking the far end of the cove, keeping boaters from venturing too near the rocky shore. It wasn't far, just about thirty yards. Last summer, he and Dani had swum the distance many times.

"Sure," she agreed, striking out with her crawl and leaving him to follow.

After the swim, they headed into shore together.

"That was just what I needed." Dani paused to shake water out of her ear. "My body feels so weightless in the ocean. I love it."

She was within arm's reach and Eliot had to make an effort not to reach out and touch her. Better yet, kiss her. Water glistened on the ends of her eyelashes, her cheeks, her lips. He wanted to taste—knew she'd be cool and sweet—

But instead, he turned and focused on the shore.

He'd lost one friend this trip already. He wouldn't be a fool and lose the one who really mattered.

⤳ ⤲

DANI WAS HAVING such a nice time that she agreed when Eliot suggested extending their holiday a few days. The weather had remained hot and she had no urge to do anything but read on the porch, float in the ocean, and enjoy the cooler evenings out on the deck with Eliot.

But the morning of their fifteenth day, she woke with a dull pain in her lower back that worried her. She went on line to confirm that this could be a sign that she was going into labor, two weeks early.

She waited until Eliot had finished his morning swim and breakfast before admitting what was happening "Would you mind driving me back to the city?"

"Of course, not. But are you sure you'll be okay for the drive? Maybe I should call an ambulance?"

"Oh, no. I'll be fine. To be on the safe side though, I'd like to see my doctor."

"I'm on it." Eliot couldn't have been more concerned if he was the father of the baby. Quickly he threw his things together, then helped her pack, too.

Looking around, she felt guilty about the mess they were

leaving behind. "Shouldn't we put away the umbrella and the outdoor cushions, at least?"

"It's just not that important. You can call the property management company for me once we're on the road. They'll take care of everything."

When Eliot said things like that, Dani became aware of the gulf between the worlds they'd been born to. His father was a successful businessman, with family money, well-placed socially. While Dani's mother had been considered high society in Marietta, Montana, Dani didn't think too many people from Seattle would be impressed with the Bramble name or legacy. As for her father, Hawksley Carrigan was a simple, hard-working ranching man. He didn't hire people to solve his problems. He fixed them himself.

But Dani had to admit she was relieved Eliot rushed her back to the city so quickly. The drive didn't help her back pains and by the time he dropped her off at the front door of the clinic, she was positive that even though her due date was two weeks away, the baby was coming that night.

It didn't though.

After a though exam, Gwen sent her home with instructions to take things easy, eat frequent, healthy snacks rather than large meals, and get lots of sleep. Eliot had stayed with her throughout the two-hours at the clinic and insisted on carrying her suitcase and book bag, not only to her condo door, but right into her bedroom. He even checked her fridge and after pronouncing it pathetic, left and then returned an hour later with three bags of healthy groceries.

"You going to be okay, now?"

"I'll be great. Thanks so much. For everything."

"Sure." He lingered at the door. "Turned out okay in the end, didn't it?"

She nodded slowly. More than okay. In fact, it felt odd to say goodbye to him when they'd spent so much time together over the past while. When Eliot leaned over to kiss her on the cheek, she had a strong urge to put her arms around him and pull him close.

Ridiculous. Thank God Eliot couldn't read her mind.

When he was gone, Dani checked her plants, relieved to see that they hadn't suffered any setbacks while she was away. She dropped over to thank Mr. Boswell, giving him a package of maple walnut fudge she'd purchased at the Farmer's Market.

A few phone messages had accumulated during the twelve days she'd been away. One from Mattie, the other from Sage. Dutifully Dani returned them both, secretly relieved when she had to leave messages for both of them.

Soon the fall session would start at the University and Portia would be back in Seattle. Dani wondered if her niece had been able to keep her secret. Perhaps she hadn't—and that was why Mattie had tried to call her?

But no. An hour later, after Dani had eaten a bowl of the lentil soup Eliot had bought for her, Mattie called back. She was full of news about Bishop Stables and the termination of her marriage to Wes. On the plus side, she'd enjoyed having the twins home from college for the summer, and there was a vague mention of a new man in her life. She didn't grill Dani at all. So Portia must have kept her word.

For her part Dani shared news of her vacation, but felt guiltily aware of all that was going unsaid on her part. She hoped her sisters would understand once they found out about the baby. Surely they'd be too happy to hold any grudges. Everything would be fine—as long as her baby was okay.

Sage called next. Dani might have found it harder to keep her secret from the sister she felt closest to, only Sage was full of details about her upcoming wedding. "I'm nervous about Dawson's mother coming." Patricia Dawson had been married either six or eight times—Dani couldn't remember which—and had dragged poor Dawson all over the country when he was growing up.

"Hopefully, she won't stay long. When is the wedding, again?"

"Second Saturday in October. Right after Homecoming. You don't have your ticket booked yet?"

Her baby would be about a month by then. Would they be ready to travel? They'd have to be, Dani realized. "I'll book today."

❧ ❦

DANI DECIDED SHE needed a good night's sleep before talking to Miriam. But early the next morning her conscience insisted that she head over to her friend's place right after breakfast. Though she knocked several times, Miriam never answered.

She tried calling next, then texting, and finally sent a

message via Facebook.

Finally, around noon, she received a terse response from Miriam.

"In Vancouver visiting my parents. Not sure when I'll be back. May put condo up for sale. Good luck with baby."

Wow.

Was that it? Did Miriam intend to end their two-year friendship with a terse three sentences on Facebook?

"Want to talk?" she messaged back.

Miriam's "No," hit the screen less than five seconds later.

Dani knew she couldn't leave things there. But she'd give Miriam a few more days to cool down before trying to contact her again. It was now time to deal with Adrian.

She hadn't thought of him as much on her holiday as she'd expected to. But now as she contemplated seeing him again her stomach felt fizzy with nerves and anticipation.

She warned herself not to get her hopes up. And she wouldn't let him control the situation, either. If he wanted to see her, this time it would be on her terms.

Just before dinner seemed like the safest time to pay him a visit. She couldn't do much about her clothes—she only had the two sundresses that fit her now—but she did take the time to wash and style her hair, and put on eye-liner, mascara and lip-gloss.

While she'd been to his house before, she took the precaution of checking Google maps before driving to his address. The house was charming, English Tudor with ivy growing attractively around the solid wood front door. She dried her damp-with-sweat left hand on the side of her dress before pressing the doorbell.

Expecting Adrian—or possibly his daughter—she was taken aback when a beautiful blonde woman with startling blue eyes opened the door.

"Yes?" The hint of a Swedish accent in the woman's voice helped Dani fill in the blanks.

"You're Olga? The nanny?"

She was tall—the same height as Dani. Slender and long-limbed. And young. Mid-twenties would be a stretch.

"I *was* the nanny, as you say. And you?"

"I—" Before she got any further, Adrian appeared in the doorway. His expression of slight annoyance quickly morphed into shock.

"Dani? What the—" He checked himself, then turned to Olga, placing a hand on her arm. "This is work, honey. Would you mind going back to the kitchen with Ava? I'll just be a few minutes."

"What the hell is going on?" Dani demanded, when instead of inviting her inside, Adrian joined her on the front stoop and closed the door.

"Come." Adrian took hold of her elbow and forcibly led her back to her car. At the driver's side door, he spoke again. "Inside."

"You can't make me." She searched his eyes for some sign of caring or warmth. But from his expression she would have guessed he was dealing firmly with a recalcitrant student.

"Please don't make a scene here on the street." He took her keys, which she was still holding in her right hand, hit "unlock," then walked around the car and got into the passenger seat.

The best option seemed to be to join him. So she got behind the wheel, making awkward adjustments for the girth of her belly. She sensed Adrian's impatience as he waited for her to get settled.

"You were never supposed to come to my house."

She'd had time to think. To process the pretty blonde's appearance at the door and her "I *was*" when Dani had presumed she was the nanny.

"You mean your Swedish girlfriend doesn't know about me? Or the fact that I'm pregnant with your child?" She felt her body shaking. She should have guessed Adrian's circumspection had little to do with his child. Almost from the beginning she'd felt like the other woman in his life. And that was exactly what she'd been.

"I'm going to tell her. Obviously."

He didn't have much choice. Not since she'd shown up at his door. But if she hadn't, Dani guessed the news might not have been forthcoming. "So how long has this been going on? You and Olga?"

"I hired her to replace the other nanny in April. We fell in love very quickly. I'm sorry I didn't end things with you right away. But then you told me you were pregnant. And I—well, obviously I didn't handle the situation very well."

Finally he was accepting at least a little bit of responsibility. "So the text messages you sent me—what were they about?"

"I wanted to see you. To tell you about Olga. We're

engaged now you see. And I also have something for you from my lawyer. You should get a second opinion, of course. But I think you'll find the payment schedule I'm proposing is on-side with Washington family law requirements."

Dani felt like a buoy out on the ocean during a big storm. The waves kept coming, pounding into her. But she stayed afloat. Riding them out.

The thing was, none of this felt like a surprise. It was as if, on some level, she'd always known Adrian was holding his heart apart from her.

Maybe it was even what had drawn her to him.

Despite her education, and the fact that she should have known better, she'd given her heart to a real asshole.

Just like dear old dad. Now, there was an insight she'd have to ponder later.

Her instinct was to demand Adrian get out of her car and keep his dirty money, too.

But he did have an obligation to their baby. And she couldn't be blind to the possibility that this child might have financial needs in excess of what she could comfortably provide.

"Fine. My attorney is Eliot Gilmore. You can instruct your lawyer to send the documentation to him."

Adrian was quiet for a long while. "That's it? All you have to say?"

She nodded.

"Look. You have every right to be angry with me. I'm sorry things worked out this way. It's not like I planned to fall in love with Olga."

She sighed, suddenly terribly weary. "I don't care about you and Olga. Just please give me your word that what happened between us won't affect our professional relationship at the University."

"It won't."

She wondered if that was true. But it was too late now for her to do anything about it. Hopefully, her work with Jenna would provide all the real job security she needed. "Great. Then I think we're done."

Oddly enough Adrian's eyes softened then. For the first time, he let his gaze drop to her belly. He looked like he was going to say something. Maybe enquire how she was feeling. But then he seemed to think better of the impulse and instead dropped a kiss on her cheek.

Dani held herself still, not reacting in any way. And then, he left.

September

WHEN THE FALL term started at the University, Dani felt disconnected from it all. Not just because she was on leave. She was drawing into herself, preparing in a very primal way for the big change that was about to happen. Like a caterpillar in the process of metamorphosis her body was changing, giving her subtle signs that it would soon be time for the baby to come.

Already, she was a week past her due date. But at her last check-up with Gwen she'd been told that the baby had dropped and it would be happening soon.

Dani could feel it. Knew it was true.

Portia was back at school and Dani felt guilty about not picking her up at the airport this time, or inviting her for dinner. But she didn't feel up to either of these things, and she hoped Portia would understand. At least it was her niece's second year. She knew her way around. And she had friends. Austin Bradshaw, Mattie informed her, was still very much in the picture. Over the summer he'd spent as much time at Bishop Stables as he could spare away from the rodeo circuit.

Funny how Portia had fallen for a rodeo cowboy—just like her dad.

Patterns. It was so easy to fall into them. Just the way she had fallen for Adrian.

Dani felt sad for herself—that she'd been so naïve. And sad for her baby, who would grow up without a dad. But she didn't feel heartbroken. Somehow her feelings for Adrian had lost their vibrancy, become shadows of love rather than the real thing. She suspected Eliot had something to do with that. But she couldn't examine that possibility too closely right now. Their friendship had deepened since Miriam's departure and their two weeks at the cottage. But it didn't seem right to consider where the changes were headed.

Her baby was all that concerned her now.

On the morning of September fifteenth, Dani woke with an urge to go for a long walk. She was out for an hour. The city was beautiful this time of year. Still green and lush, but the days were getting shorter. Winter was inevitable. Before too long gray days and rain would replace all this beautiful sunshine.

By the time she returned to the condo, she knew the bands of muscles tightening around her abdomen were telling her something. No longer just uncomfortable, they were becoming painful. And closer together.

She had a suitcase by her door. All she had to do was call the taxi.

Eliot had told her to phone him when the time came. Didn't matter if he was at work, or in court, in a meeting or at lunch, he'd come and take her to the hospital. He understood she didn't want him with her during the birth. But he wanted to be close at hand.

Dani appreciated his offer. A lot. But deep inside she felt that this was a journey for her to take on her own. So she watered her plants, then went down to the lobby to wait for her taxi.

Before long she was at the clinic, being examined by a nurse who asked her why she had waited so long. No sooner was the question asked, than Dani's water broke.

And it all happened quickly after that.

Her doctor was her lifeline, arriving just when the pain was at its worst. "How are you doing, Dani? Your nurses tell me you're progressing quickly."

"If that means it hurts like hell, they're right." Dani ground out the words, taking hold of the hand Gwen offered and squeezing it tightly.

"Unusual for the labor to progress this quickly for a first baby. But it's going to be okay. Is there anyone you want me to call?"

"No." Inside Dani was cursing every decision she'd made leading up to this day. Having unprotected sex with Adrian the night of the Christmas party. Keeping the baby. Not going for the amniocentesis. Not reaching out to one of her sisters. If she hadn't been so stubborn Sage, or Mattie or even Callan would be with her right now. And it would have helped, to have someone who loved her.

She hadn't understood that until this moment. Notwithstanding the medical personal continually checking her, how alone she would feel.

Time passed. Seconds or minutes, she couldn't tell. Several nurses were hovering, checking vitals, preparing something out of her field of vision. Then Gwen asked her to put her feet into the stirrups.

"You're fully dilated Dani. It's time to push."

One of the nurses stayed by her side. Her name was Cindy and she was very kind. She coached her through it, telling her when to breathe, when to push, when to relax.

There was terrible pain, and a feeling of urgency. The baby was coming but it was pulling her apart. "I can't!"

"Yes, you can." Cindy's voice was gentle and assured. Like Dani's mother's.

Yes. You. Can. The words ran through Dani's head, over and over and the cycle of pushing, breathing and relaxing went on and on and on.

And then it was "One last push, Dani. We see your baby's head—"

And whoosh. It was done.

"You have a beautiful baby girl."

Dani didn't have the strength to lift her head. A girl. She hadn't admitted it until now, but she'd been hoping for a daughter. "Let me—" She wanted to ask to hold her baby, but her voice gave out.

Someone new came into the room and introduced themselves. She tried to focus on the name. Dr. Wittingdale?

"How are you doing?" Gwen came to the side of her bed and gave her shoulder a squeeze. "We just need to deliver the placenta. Try to relax."

Dani did. She was so relieved the pain was over. She had a baby. She'd done it. That Dr. Wittingdale—had he said he was a pediatrician? He must be checking her baby. When he was finished, maybe they'd let Dani hold her.

Time went by. Her brain was too foggy to process how much. She heard murmured voices from one corner. A nurse was washing her up, raising her bed so she was in a semi-seated position. Then Gwen was back, surgical mask removed and smiling softly.

"There is good news. Your baby's heart and lungs are fine. She scored a nine on the Apgar test. A healthy, strong little thing. Six pounds, ten ounces."

Dani felt another contraction. This one of her heart. She wanted to pray. But she could tell it was too late. She pushed her upper body away from the bed so she could study her doctor's familiar face. "But?"

"Well, Dani, I've called in Dr. Wittingdale. He's one of our top pediatricians. And he suspects—well, he's quite sure—that your daughter has Down Syndrome."

Unexpectedly, Dani felt angry. "You can't know that for sure."

Her doctor didn't seem perturbed by her harsh words. "No. Not until we get the results from the blood test."

Dani tried to think of something logical to say. But every thought she had seemed to run up against a brick wall. In the end all she could manage was, "I want to hold her."

"Of course."

In stepped the nice nurse. Cindy. She had Dani's baby already bundled into a cotton blanket. "And you can try to nurse her, too, if you can manage. Sometimes babies with Down Syndrome have a little trouble."

"That hasn't been proven, yet." Dani found herself snapping again.

But as soon as she saw the little face, the dark, almond-shaped eyes, she knew.

And in her heart, she admitted it was no less than what she'd expected. It was why she'd avoided the extra tests, because she'd known what they would find and the predicament they would put her in.

She hadn't wanted to make that choice, deciding to end the life of her baby.

But by avoiding the test, she had made a choice. To bring this child into the world.

And now it would be all up to her, to protect this sweet baby and love her. To make a home for her. To be her family.

&〜 〜&

ELIOT PICKED UP two orders of Thai salad on his way home from work. Lately, he and Dani had been having most of their evening meals together. Their friendship had continued to grow tighter in the wake of Miriam's departure from Seattle. Which showed every sign of being permanent. Just that weekend there'd been an open house at her condo unit.

She was selling.

He felt guilty, but relieved. It wasn't often a guy had to kick a naked woman out of his bed. Conversation after-the-fact was bound to be awkward.

It wasn't that he didn't care about Miriam anymore. But she'd crossed too many lines.

He tapped on Dani's door, intending to drop off the

food, then go home and change before joining her. When she didn't answer, he modified his plans and went home first. Once he was in casual shorts and T-shirt, he sent her a text message.

Ten minutes later, he tried her door again.

By now he wasn't worried about the Thai food getting cold. She was having the baby. He just knew it. Still, he remained calm enough to phone the clinic and confirm that she'd been admitted. She had. Eight hours ago.

☙ ❧

CINDY, THE NICE nurse, turned out to be around Dani's age. She had two children at home, six-year-old twins. "My sister, Mattie, had twins. The first six months were really tough. Mom spent a lot of time helping her. My family lives in Montana," she added, as if that were important.

Dani and the baby had been moved to a different room, where a curtain separated them from another new mom and her baby. The father had just left, taking with him a petulant two-year-old who didn't seem thrilled at the idea of a new sibling.

"Will your mom be coming to Seattle to help you?" Cindy asked. She was changing Baby Carrigan's diaper now, following a somewhat successful first feeding.

"No. My Mom died in a ranching accident many years ago."

"I'm sorry."

"Yes. Me, too."

"Here's your baby, all clean and ready to sleep. Do you

want me to put her in the bassinette so you can get some rest?"

"No. I'll hold her."

Cindy withdrew, closing the curtain behind her. Dani gazed down at her daughter's tiny nose, pursed mouth, and chin no bigger than a button. This was their first moment alone, and Dani was surprised that she didn't feel afraid. All she felt was a huge amount of tenderness and love.

Dani was proud of the fact that her baby had latched on and suckled, even if for only five minutes. Lots of babies with Down Syndrome had problems breastfeeding. She hoped it was an omen. That her daughter would be able to thrive in this world, despite her disability.

But the future was something Dani couldn't think too much about right now. She'd handle life minute by minute for next few days. At some point, when she didn't feel so overwhelmed, she'd catch her breath. Maybe then the reality of the situation would finally sink in.

For half an hour Dani was content to hold her baby and watch her sleep. But then she realized she still hadn't told anyone, not any of her friends or family, where she was and what had happened. Eliot might even be worried about her, since he usually checked in with her a few times a day.

But before she spoke to anyone, she supposed the father of her baby ought to be the first to receive the news. Gently Dani settled her baby in the bassinette, then dug her phone out of her purse. Given the nature of their most recent conversation, she felt no qualms at all notifying Adrian of his daughter's birth by text message.

For once he responded almost immediately. "Everything okay?"

It was a complicated question in this situation, but Dani felt justified in responding with a simple, "Yes."

"Good. I'll see you shortly."

Now that surprised her even more than the quick answer to her text. Their agreement was still in the hands of their lawyers, but essentially it granted Dani sole custody and laid out Adrian's financial obligations. Provisions had been made so that with sufficient notice, Adrian could visit the baby if he so wished. But she hadn't expected he would 'so wish' very often.

Dani had every intention of calling Eliot next. Then Portia and Jenna, and maybe even Miriam, though her friend hadn't responded to any of her messages since she'd left Seattle.

But the adrenaline rush she'd felt after the birth had trailed off, and she was suddenly sapped of energy. She'd just close her eyes for a bit. Only for ten minutes or so—

❧ ❧

SHE MUST HAVE slept longer than she intended, because the next thing Dani knew she sensed someone else in the room. She opened her eyes to find Adrian peering through the curtain. Based on the way he was dressed, a light gray blazer over dark jeans, with a button-down, blue shirt, she guessed he'd come directly from work.

"What time is it?" She sat up and tucked her hair behind her ears. She must look like a mess.

"Seven."

"In the evening?"

He smiled. "You must have had a long day." He set a small African violet plant on the window sill, then came and kissed her forehead, withdrawing quickly after the fleeting contact.

He looked as handsome as ever, but somehow whatever qualities had previously drawn her to him had lost their power. Today all she noticed was that he seemed older than she recalled. And however he'd spent the summer, exercise didn't seem to have been involved.

"She's over there." Dani nodded at the bassinette. "Go ahead and pick her up if you'd like." She thought about warning him. But her mind was still foggy from sleep and she couldn't think of what to say anyway. She hadn't expected him to visit or to show any interest in the baby.

But he did. Tenderly he lifted the little bundle and brought her up to cradle in his arms. "She sure has a lot of hair."

"Yes." Dark and wavy, like her daddy.

"She has your nose," he said. "Oh, she's waking up now. Look at those eyes—"

Suddenly, he tensed. He looked from the baby, to Dani, then back at the baby. "Oh my God, Dani. I don't know how to tell you this, but I think—"

"I know, Adrian. Our baby has Down Syndrome, also known as Trisomy 21." Unwittingly, she adopted a professorial tone to relay the information, as if by keeping her voice business-like, she could negate all the emotions that came with the information.

Quickly, as if she were infectious, he placed the baby back in her bassinette. "How did this happen? There are tests. You should have been warned."

"They did discover certain abnormalities during my ultrasound. I decided against further testing." She plucked at the sheet covering her body, her emotions oddly dulled. A defensive mechanism, no doubt.

"Why the hell would you do that? And why wasn't I consulted?"

"Why should I? You never once offered to come to a medical appointment with me. Or called to check how I was doing. Or expressed any interest in the health of the baby."

"But I was still the father. I had a right to be included in this decision."

"It has nothing to do with you. I'm the one who's going to raise her."

"While I'm stuck footing the bill."

"Really? That's all you care about?" She'd instructed Eliot to ask only for the minimum child support required under the law, even though Eliot had told her he could probably make a case for more.

"I wouldn't have minded so much if the kid had a chance at a good life. But this baby is never going to grow up to be a productive member of society. You're going to be saddled with looking after her all your life. And frankly, I could think of a lot better things to do with my money than—"

"Enough." Their argument was interrupted as Eliot

stepped into the curtained area. His expression was hard, and his hands were in fists as he squared off against Adrian. "You better leave."

"Who the hell are you to tell me to leave?"

Dani wanted to say that he was her friend. That he was the one person she could count on. The truth was, she couldn't remember ever being so happy to see anyone as she was to see Eliot right then.

But Eliot didn't give her a chance to say anything. Two long steps had him towering over the shorter man. "I'm Dani's friend and attorney. And I believe the legal agreement between you requires twenty-four hour notice should you want to spend time with your daughter—though based on what I just heard, I'm guessing you won't be exercising that particular right very often."

"You can't be much of a friend if you weren't able to talk her out of this madness. Have you seen this baby? Any reasonable woman would have sought proper testing and then terminated the pregnancy once she found out it had Down Syndrome. Out of kindness to the child, if nothing else."

Her numbness was wearing off. Dani could feel the weight of her heart growing with each vile word Adrian spoke. Maybe he was right. What chance did their child have in this world, if her own father couldn't love her?

"You don't know Dani at all, do you?" Eliot sounded incredulous. "I'm sure many women would do exactly what you just said. And that would be their right, absolutely. But that's not Dani's way."

"What do you know about Dani's way?" Adrian made the words sound like a sneer.

"She's got a tender heart. Looks out for the underdog. Hey—she slept with you, right, the poor widowed father left to raise his daughter alone?"

"You bastard." Adrian's sneer turned to a scowl. "You know nothing about me or my relationship with Dani. None of this is any of your business."

"Taking care of Dani—her legal interests—is absolutely my business. Now get out before I call security."

But he didn't need to call anyone. A nurse had been alerted by the commotion and was drawing open the curtains and frowning. "What's going on?"

Eliot jerked a thumb at Adrian, then pulled out a wad of tissues from the package on the bedside table and dabbed away tears Dani hadn't realized she'd shed.

"I want him to go," Dani said, pointing at Adrian, too.

"I'll gladly leave this disaster zone." Adrian shot her one more disgusted look, then exited.

The nurse eyed Dani keenly. "Are you okay now, dear?"

She managed to nod.

"Hit the button if anyone bothers you again."

Once the nurse was gone, Eliot snorted. "What an effing jerk."

Dani could have kissed him for saying that. But instead, to her utter dismay, she burst into tears.

❧ ❧

IT WAS A hell of a thing, to realize you were in love with a woman on the day she gave birth to another man's child. Eliot had wanted to attack Adrian physically when he'd overheard the other man berating Dani about the baby. In his life he'd never hated anyone, not even in heated courtroom battles, but in that instant he'd hated Adrian.

And a second later, he'd understood why. He'd been kidding himself about the nature of his feelings toward Dani. They went far beyond friendship. He was crazy about her, and he couldn't even say when it had happened. Only that it had. The Down Syndrome, yes that had come as a shock. But all that mattered to him now was comforting Dani.

He longed to gather her into his arms. But she'd curled up into a ball on the hospital bed, sobbing like her heart was breaking and undoubtedly it was. Maybe she needed this cry.

Awkwardly he patted her back, then went to see the baby. Wide, almond-shaped eyes glanced in his direction as he bent over the bassinette. "Hello, sweetie. Quite the crazy world you've stepped into today."

She blinked, then her eyelids fluttered and she drifted into sleep.

He touched her cheek, amazed at the softness. Then went back to sit by the side of Dani's bed. "Hey. It's going to be okay. Don't let him get to you."

"B-but maybe he's right."

"That asshole? I doubt it."

Dani made a choking sound, half laugh, half sob. "I t-thought if it happened, if she was born with Down Syndrome, that we'd be able to handle it. T-that she would still be happy. Have a good life, you know?"

"And she still can. That professor of yours may be smart about some things, but he's no expert on Down Syndrome."

"How do you know?"

"Every child with the syndrome is unique. Just like kids without the syndrome are, too. No way can you predict the future for any child when they're one day old." He passed her another wad of tissues.

"That sounds like something my mother would have said. Thanks Eliot. I-I'm sorry you had to walk into all this drama."

He smoothed her hair away from her face, wondering if she had any idea how he felt. He couldn't imagine his feelings were returned. Not yet, anyway. But maybe one day, he'd have a chance with her. Until then he'd be what she really needed right now. A friend.

"I'm afraid, Eliot. What if I'm not strong enough to be the mother my baby needs?"

"You'll be strong enough," he promised. And if she wasn't, he'd be there to help her.

❧ ❦

ELIOT DIDN'T LEAVE the clinic until Dani had calmed down, fed the baby again, then fallen back to sleep. It was dark, almost nine o'clock. As he walked toward his SUV, he glanced at his phone and saw Nick Greenway had called.

What the hell. He decided to phone him back. "What's up?"

"Lizbeth has decided to file for divorce again."

"I heard."

"Well. Can't you stop her? You managed to talk her out of it last time."

"Maybe that was a mistake on my part."

"It wasn't. She loves me. And I still love her."

"Even though she cheated on you?" Eliot had reached his SUV. Instead of getting inside, he leaned against the hood and stared back at the clinic, trying to count the windows and figure out which one belonged to Dani's room.

"Yeah. Even though."

"Then, what's the problem?"

"She wants me to treat that baby like it's mine. And I can't."

Eliot had no more patience for this. "Look, Nick. Do you love her or not?"

"I do. I told you. But how can I help raise a child that some other guy fathered?"

There was Dani's room. Eliot could see the plant in the window. An African violet for her collection. He suspected she wouldn't love this healthy one nearly as much as she did the scraggly ones she'd bought back from near death.

"You can do it if you love her enough, Nick. But that's for you to decide."

Eliot already knew his answer. If Dani wanted him— he'd be there. For her and the baby.

⤸ ❧

TEN DAYS AFTER the birth of her daughter, Dani was a wreck. She couldn't get her baby to settle for more than a few hours at a time. And during those brief down periods when she ought to have been sleeping herself and gathering strength, she ended up crying half the time. Consequently, she was exhausted, and the place was a mess. Good thing she'd stocked up on the essentials before the birth, because she hadn't been able to go for groceries, hadn't even made it out of the condo at all, except for the baby's one-week check-up. And she'd been fifteen minutes late for that.

Breastfeeding was an all-consuming routine when your baby wanted to eat every three hours. Dani ate her own meals on the run and settled for sponge bathing rather than showers, because they were faster.

Eliot had driven them home from the clinic and had come by a few times since, but she'd asked him to stop. She didn't want him to see her like this. Not just incompetent, but actually falling apart.

With each passing day she became more convinced that Adrian had been right—and she'd made nothing but bad decisions since the day she found out she was pregnant. Oh, she loved her baby, thought she was the most precious creature ever. But she hated to think of all the vile comments, the rejections and disappointments that would surely come in her child's future. The vehemence of Adrian's anger, the palpable disgust he'd had for their baby, were stamped in her memory. And he was the father. How could she possibly expect strangers to behave any kinder?

Many times a day Dani longed to reach out to one of her sisters. But how could she ask for their help now, when she'd shut them out for so long? Her decision to keep her pregnancy secret was another of her deep regrets. It had been a form of repression—not talking about the baby had allowed her to push the possibility of complications to the back of her mind. She couldn't believe how illogical she'd been. As if by ignoring the problem it would somehow go away.

But it hadn't. The abnormalities that had been noticed in her first ultrasound had been real. Her baby was the living proof.

And now they were both going to have to live with the consequences, but Dani didn't know how. At their one week check-up, she'd been told they were very fortunate that her baby hadn't been born with any of the heart problems or eating difficulties that often plagued children with Down Syndrome.

At this point she didn't feel fortunate. And she doubted her ability to handle a normal child, let alone one with extra challenges.

She'd notified Portia, Jenna and a few other friends and colleagues of her baby's arrival by email, but hadn't answered any of their replies. Somehow she was going to have to tell them about the Down Syndrome. But how? The effort was totally beyond her right now.

The sheets on her bed hadn't been changed in weeks and they desperately needed washing. Dani didn't care, however, as she fell face first onto the mattress after an early morning feeding. She hadn't even changed the baby's diaper this time. Surely one skipped diaper change wouldn't hurt anything.

But when she awoke a few hours later, to her daughter's angry cries, Dani saw the beginning of a pink rash on her little bottom and felt submersed with guilt. She was terrible at this. Just terrible. After cleaning her baby and applying some ointment, she gave her another feeding, then, cradling her close to her chest went around closing all the window blinds against the early morning light. She was beginning to hate sunshine because it only allowed her to see what a mess her place was. She'd even turned away the cleaning service this week because she was ashamed to let them inside.

Dani prided herself on being a smart woman. So how had her life come to this?

❧ ❧

THOUGH FILES WERE piling up on his desk, and his unanswered emails and phone calls were mounting, Eliot couldn't concentrate. He was beyond worried. For a week Dani hadn't been letting him in when he knocked on her door. His text messages and phone calls were also ignored. All he'd had from her was one simple line: "Need some time to adjust."

Trouble was, he didn't think she was adjusting. She needed help, but was too proud, or ashamed, or something to let anyone in. This was all thanks to that tirade in the hospital by that stupid jerk former boyfriend. He'd been totally off base, but somehow Adrian's words had gotten to Dani, undermining her already shaky confidence in her abilities as a mother.

Even worse, Adrian had accused her of being cruel by bringing a child with disabilities into the world. In normal circumstances Dani would have seen that Adrian was the cruel one. But in her tired and vulnerable state she'd taken his words too much to heart.

Paige was at his door, wearing a dress covered in daisies and bearing a stack of paperwork he feared was for him.

"Thought I'd let you know the Greenway divorce has been halted."

"Has it?" He wondered if his conversation with Nick the other week had been instrumental. "Well, I wish them the best."

"Is something wrong? You seem a little distracted lately."

He shook his head. "Sorry. A friend is in a jam and I haven't been thinking straight lately. I wish I could do something to help her."

"This friend wouldn't be Dani Carrigan?"

He and Paige didn't talk about their personal lives often. But over the years they'd become familiar with each other's families and close friends. He'd told her Miriam had moved out of Seattle. And she knew about Dani's pregnancy, too.

"Her baby was born with Down Syndrome. I don't think she's told any of her family or other friends. She's just holed up in her condo trying to handle everything herself."

"Oh, gosh. Poor woman." Paige dropped off the papers, then sat in one of the chairs opposite his desk.

"I want to help, but I don't know how." He was a man who needed a plan. Once he knew what to do, he could make it happen.

Paige tilted her head thoughtfully. "Well, she probably needs help with cleaning and with meals. But more than that, she could use someone to talk to."

"I'm not so sure about that." She sure didn't seem interested in talking to him lately.

"Do you remember the Churchills? You did some estate planning for them, six years ago after their second son was born."

Eliot's mind was blank. Why was she bringing up a case from so long ago? And then it came to him. "You're brilliant, Paige."

She left the chair with a smile. "I like to think so."

❧ ❦

WHEN SHE HEARD the knock at her door, the only reason Dani knew it was early afternoon was because she'd heard the noon hour news a while ago. She'd turned on the TV that morning, just to remind herself that the entire world hadn't ended. Only hers.

Go away Eliot, she said to herself as she finished fastening the baby's new diaper. All traces of the rash were gone now and she was super vigilant about keeping her baby's bottom dry. There was some comfort in knowing that at least she was capable of doing the basics for her daughter. Feeding her and keeping her clean. Holding her close and telling her she was loved.

If only that could be enough.

There was a repeat of the knocking, a little louder and longer this time.

Darn it, Eliot. She put the baby into her portable bassinette—she was just too tiny for the big crib. Plus Dani liked to keep her near, at all times. "Be right back, sweetie."

She washed her hands and winced at her reflection. Ugh. Her total beauty routine these days consisted of brushing her teeth and running a damp facecloth over her body in the morning. Not only did she look rough, she suspected she didn't smell that great either.

For the third time there was knocking at the door. Louder. And it didn't stop.

Dani marched to the entranceway where she unlocked the deadbolt, but kept the safety chain attached. Holding the door ajar less than an inch she said, "Eliot, this isn't a good time. I'm trying to get the baby to sleep."

"Uh, sorry Dani. I'm not Eliot. This is Fredrick Bowman. I'm sorry to disturb you but if I could just have a minute—"

Oh my lord. Mr. Bowman? Something must be wrong for him to have pounded on her door like that. The most he'd ever done before was give a timid knock. Quickly she unlatched the door. "Are you okay?"

"Huh? Oh, yes, of course I am." He looked at her with obvious concern. "Are you?"

She brushed a hand over her hair, then when she saw his gaze slip past her, to the mess in her living room, she stepped out to the hall, partially closing the door behind her. "I'm afraid I can't invite you in. The place is a disaster zone."

Mr. Bowman glanced down the hall to her left, then cleared his throat. "I heard you'd had your baby. And I don't want to be a bother. But you've been so kind to me, I wanted to do something to help." He held out his hands, palm side up. "But I can't cook, as you know, so I couldn't bring over any food. And then it hit me. Maybe you could use some help with the baby. So you could do things like go out shopping and—" he glanced at her hair, "—maybe go to the hair salon or whatever young ladies like you need to do."

Dani didn't know whether to laugh or cry at the idea of leaving her baby with sweet, old Mr. Bowman. "I'm not quite at the stage where I could leave the baby with a sitter. But it's very nice of you to offer."

"Oh. I didn't explain. I'm not—" His gaze shifted to the side again. "I mean, I could hardly offer my own services. But I have a widowed friend whose daughter and her family recently moved away. She told me she'd love to go back to work as a nanny to a nice family. And as it happens, she's at my place right now, so I thought—maybe you would like to meet her?"

Something was wrong here. Why would Mr. Bowman suddenly show up at her door offering the services of a friend who just happened to be looking for babysitting? And he kept looking down the hall—toward Eliot's door.

"Did Eliot put you up to this?"

"Um. Well."

She'd thought so. "I'm sure you mean well, Mr. Bowman. But—"

Before she could finish her sentence, Eliot came out into the hall with a woman who looked to be in her late fifties. She had short, salt-and-pepper hair, a pleasant face and a figure that was trim despite the fact that she didn't seem to have a waistline.

"I'm Mrs. Muddle, dear. It's so nice to meet you. I hear

you've had quite the few weeks. I remember what it was like when my first child was born."

Dani looked beyond her, to Eliot, who was leaning against his door frame, watching with more than a little satisfaction. She hated that he was seeing her this way, her greasy hair, her shirt spotted with breast milk and baby spit, mis-matched socks on her feet because she'd put them on in the dark and hadn't been bothered to change them later in the day when she'd realized her mistake.

Mrs. Muddle—was that really her name?—pushed open Dani's door and disappeared inside. Mr. Bowman was already at his own door, and a second later was gone, too.

"That was diabolical. Tricking me with dear, old Mr. Bowman that way."

"Couldn't think of another way of getting you to open your door."

She couldn't believe the way Eliot was looking at her, with so much warmth and concern. Was he really not disgusted at the sight of her? "I know I look awful. I've been afraid to take a shower in case the baby started crying and I couldn't hear her."

"You should have called me."

She glanced away. She knew he would have helped, if she'd asked him to. But she'd thought if she could look after the baby by herself she'd be able to prove that Adrian was wrong, that she hadn't made a mistake, that she was going to be a good mother, after all.

But she'd failed.

"I hired Mrs. Muddle from an agency. You have her

services for two weeks."

"I—" How could she tell him she didn't want any help, when it was so obvious she needed it. "How did you find her?"

"Paige contacted one of the top nanny agencies in town and then personally checked her references. She's top-notch, I promise. Just give her a chance, okay?"

Dani sighed. Again, she couldn't see how she could say no.

"She's already been paid to stay until six tonight. If you're not happy, I'll tell her not to bother coming back tomorrow."

"All right. Thank you."

She stepped back inside but before she could shut the door, Eliot said, "Oh. One more thing."

Feeling trepidatious, she waited, eyebrows arched expectantly.

"I've got someone I want you to meet tonight. You can expect us at seven."

⊱ ⊰

"MRS. MUDDLE?" DANI couldn't see any sign of the nanny Eliot had hired in her living area or the adjoining kitchen. Hearing the sound of the washing machine, she checked the laundry room across the hall from the half bath. The washer was going, but no sign of the nanny.

Dani glanced into her study, then the nursery, and finally found Mrs. Muddle in the master bedroom, pulling the sheets and pillowcases from her bed. In her portable crib by the window, the baby was peacefully sleeping.

"I do light-housekeeping as well as child care duties. I put in the load of whites I found in your hamper. I'll do these sheets and then the towels. If you want to take a shower, I'll listen for the wee one. She's sound asleep; I'm sure you can take your time."

Overwhelmed at having her life so invaded by a stranger, Dani was speechless for a long moment. But what the heck. Her references had been checked, and Dani had a lot of faith in both Eliot and his assistant.

"You'll call me if she wakes up?"

"Right away. I promise."

"Well, a shower sure would feel great."

After ten glorious minutes under her ceiling mounted rainfall showerhead, during which time she lathered her hair twice and shaved her armpits, Dani turned off the water, then stuck her head out of the shower. Hearing silence, she decided to turn the water back on for another glorious five minutes.

Wrapped in a towel she went to check on the baby, only to find that the nanny had moved the portable crib to the kitchen—"So I can keep my eyes on her while I tidy up a bit."

Dani eyed her kitchen in amazement. So far Mrs. Muddle's "tidy up a bit" involved loading and starting the dishwasher, washing down all the counters and scouring the sink.

"Wow. The place looks a lot better all ready."

"I love a good challenge, dear. Now you go get dressed

and dry your hair. I'll let you know as soon as I hear a peep."

Dani wasn't yet into her regular clothes, but she managed to get into the jeans she'd bought with Miriam when she'd first found out she was pregnant. The reminder of a friend who'd once been such a big part of her life made her sad. Miriam still hadn't responded to the email announcing her baby's birth. It seemed Miriam was cutting her and Eliot out of her life for good.

After drying her hair, Dani decided it would be good for her morale to put on some mascara and lip gloss. It was a relief to see her old self staring back from the mirror when she was done.

And then, with perfect timing, the baby let out a squawk. A sound Dani was learning to interpret that meant she was waking up and would soon demand to be fed. She hurried to the kitchen only to find that Mrs. Muddle had beaten her to the portable crib.

She assumed Eliot had warned her about the Down Syndrome, but she was still anxious to see how the nanny would react. In the past few weeks, her baby's face had filled out a little and now Dani could see even more that she had the classic flatter face, as well as the slanted eyes of a Down baby. Would Mrs. Muddle see her as less cute or loveable than a regular baby?

But if she did, she showed no signs of it.

"Come here you little sweet pea." Mrs. Muddle lifted her gently, then cuddled the baby to her chest. "Nothing like the smell of a newborn baby." She started a rocking motion, the cleaning of the kitchen suddenly not even the slightest of concerns.

Dani watched, bemused, and a little bereft, that a stranger could provide the comfort she'd assumed only she, the mother, could offer. Then, seeing that her baby was perfectly happy and that Mrs. Muddle seemed to be enjoying her chance to hold the baby, she decided to go to her office and do a quick check of e-mails.

Twenty minutes later, Mrs. Muddle came to the doorway. "I believe sweet pea would like to eat now."

Dani went to sit in the rocking chair in the nursery to breastfeed her baby. When she was finished, Dani gave her a sponge bath and changed her into a clean sleeper for the night. Miraculously, the bureau had been restocked with clean onesies and sleepers Mrs. Muddle must have already run through the drier and then folded.

By the time she'd settled the baby in her portable crib again, Mrs. Muddle had a cheese and herb omelet, toast and tea waiting for her.

"I hope you don't mind, dear, but I phoned in a grocery list. You're shockingly low on provisions. They'll be delivered tomorrow at nine."

"You are amazing. Absolutely amazing." Gone was every last one of Dani's reservations about hiring a nanny. She hadn't realized until that minute how starving she felt.

"Just doing my job. And I must say, it's been very satisfying. What a sweet daughter you have."

"Thank you."

Mrs. Muddle nodded. "It's a bit past six, so I'll be leaving now. I'll be here tomorrow before the groceries arrive. Don't worry if you have a rough night. You'll be able to have a nice long nap tomorrow now that you've seen I know a thing or two about babies. I did have four of my own." Mrs. Muddle winked, then briskly went on her way.

UNTIL SHE HEARD the knock at her door, Dani had forgotten Eliot's promise to visit—and bring guests—at seven o'clock. Thanks to Mrs. Muddle she felt almost her old self again. But the prospect of visitors made her want to hide her head under the covers again.

But Eliot had sent her Mrs. Muddle. So she owed him.

It was still with some reluctance, however, that she opened the door to him.

God he looked good. So good. Long and lean, elegantly well-dressed. His quirky smile sparked something like joy in her heart and she couldn't help smiling back at him in return.

"I see Mrs. Muddle agrees with you."

"I wouldn't be surprised if you told me she appeared out of the sky one day, floating down with an umbrella."

He laughed. "That good, huh?"

"Totally changed my life. In just one day." She opened the door wider to let him in, and only then noticed a woman and a little boy standing about three feet away from him.

He gestured them forward. "Dani, this is Jess Churchill and her son Cole. I asked them to come and talk to you about their experiences the past six years."

Dani shook hands with the mother who looked about

Mattie's age, maybe a few years older. She was tall and very slender, with large brown eyes and a broad, engaging smile.

"It's nice to meet you, Dani. This is my son Cole. He turned six this year." She pulled the boy, who'd been hanging back a little, out in front of her. As he gave Dani a shy smile, the purpose of this visit became very clear.

Cole had Down Syndrome, too. Just like her own baby.

Dani invited them in and offered to make tea or coffee, but Jess and Cole only wanted water and Eliot waved off any refreshments at all. They sat on the white leather sectional, which Dani was beginning to realize was a piece of furniture she would soon be looking to sell. White furniture and children were not a good mix.

"Where is your baby?" Jess asked her.

"She just fell asleep in the portable crib in my room. Would you like to see her?"

"Oh, I hate to disturb a sleeping baby."

"I don't mind." Dani was suddenly anxious to have her daughter close to her. The little sweetie didn't even open her eyes when Dani eased her out of the crib and into her arms. The baby's warmth felt reassuring against her chest and Dani held her close before taking a breath and re-entering the living room.

"Jess and her husband are clients of mine," Eliot explained, after he and Jess had both taken a moment to admire the baby. "They came to me after Cole's birth for some estate planning."

"We were concerned about what would happen to our children if something happened to us while they were so young. And then having a child with special needs made us worry all the more."

"How many children do you have?"

"Three. Cole has an older brother and sister."

"Mom?" Cole interjected with a whisper. "I'm bored. Can I have the mini pad?" When she didn't react, he added, "Please, Mom?"

"Sure, honey." Jess pulled a mini i-Pad from her purse and Dani was impressed to see the little boy touch, swipe and scroll his way around the screen, like an expert.

"Wow, he knows what he's doing."

"Yes. Like all little kids he loves technology. That's why Eliot wanted us to come and see you today." Jess reached across to touch Dani's arm. "We didn't know what to expect when Cole was born. We couldn't help but worry. But then we joined a support group and learned that most children with Down Syndrome learn to talk, walk, read and play just like other children—though it may take them a little longer. We have Cole enrolled in a special school where he's thriving."

"Mom! I got a high score!" Cole held out his hand for his mother to give him a high-five.

The way Jess smiled at her son told Dani even more than her words had. She could see how much this child was loved and cared for. Just as she could see that while Cole looked a little different—his thick glasses magnified his almond-shaped eyes and his limbs and fingers were stubby—he was a happy child.

The conversation flowed after that. Dani had so many questions and wished they could stay longer. But after half-an-hour the games had stopped entertaining Cole and he started to get a little whiney.

"He's tired," Jess explained. "We really should be going."

But she left Dani with contact information for a support group, as well as for the nursery and grade schools that she'd found so wonderful for Cole.

"Thank you so much for coming." Dani was touched when Jess replied by giving her a hug.

"Call me anytime if you need someone to talk to."

"I'm going to walk them out to their car and then I'll be right back," Eliot said, on his way out the door.

"I'll leave the door unlocked so you can come in. I'm going to give the baby a feeding and change her diaper."

Ten minutes later, Dani heard Eliot return. She was in the rocking chair, nursing the baby, but her daughter was so drowsy, she decided she might as well change her diaper and put her back in the crib. She was just settling her into the covers, when Eliot tapped on the bedroom door.

"You okay in here?"

"Yes. Almost done." Dani gave her daughter a kiss, then turned to Eliot. "I don't know how to thank you."

"The Churchills are quite the family."

"Yes." She'd been in such a black hole since Adrian's tirade at the hospital. So sure that she was the most selfish and stupid woman in the world. "Meeting Jess and Cole—it's really given me hope."

"I'm glad."

Something in his voice made her look at him more close-ly. She felt heat rising up between them, an awareness of feelings that had been suppressed for a very long time. Did he have any idea how attractive she found him? How much she respected and trusted and just plain liked him?

"You're such a great guy. Too bad you're a confirmed bachelor."

One corner of his mouth turned up. "Is that how you see me?"

She shrugged. "Dating a different woman every month. What else could I think?"

"I haven't dated anyone for a while now."

It was true. She tried to remember the last time she'd heard his voice switch to "charming" mode when he answered his phone, or seen him come home bleary-eyed after a late evening out.

"What's happening to you?" she said, trying to keep a teasing tone in her voice. Trying not to let him see how much she cared about his answer.

"I've been wondering the same thing. I thought maybe I was tired of the whole dating scene. But then I realized it was more complicated than that. I was in love."

"In love."

He nodded. "In love with someone who'd been right under my nose for the past two years. But by the time I realized how I felt, she was dating someone else. Then, pregnant and having his baby."

Dani felt as if the room had started spinning. All these crazy, wonderful things. Was Eliot really saying them—to her?

"I can't even understand what I saw in Aidan anymore."

"I can. He was new to Seattle and the University. A grieving widower. A single father. Of course you were drawn to him, Dani. You wanted to heal him, the way you try to heal all the broken people and things in your life."

She wanted to tease him about being an armchair psychiatrist, but his assessment rang true. She could see the pattern herself now, not just with Adrian, but with other men she'd dated, what her college and grad school friends had called her "fix-it projects."

"The question on the table now," Eliot continued. "Is whether I have a hope in hell with you? My timing isn't good. I get that. But I can wait."

The steady light in his eyes told her that he could. And would.

"No waiting necessary. I was already crazy about you this summer, when we were at the cottage. But—as you say—the timing was terrible."

Eliot held out his hands and when she reached for them, he pulled her in nice and close and kissed her. She'd been nervous about this kiss, wondering if the sexual pull between them could possibly match the emotional connection they already shared.

It did.

❧ ❦

IN HIS WILDEST dreams Eliot hadn't expected the plan he'd concocted with Paige that morning to turn out this well. Mrs. Muddle. Jess and Cole Churchill. And now this.

Them.

Kissing in the hallway. Dani tasting and feeling like the woman he wanted to be with for the rest of his life. He ached to pick her up and carry her to the bed. The way she was kissing him back, she felt the same way.

"I never thought I could feel so sexual right after having a baby," she marveled.

"Did your doctor happen to mention how long before you'll be ready for sex?"

"Four to six weeks." She shrugged. "Give or take."

He groaned. "So it's just kissing for now—"

She took his hand. "Let's make out on the couch like teenagers."

"I'm too old for this." But it turned out he wasn't. Because he couldn't stop touching her. Kissing her. Marveling in the fact that she loved him back. How could he be so lucky? They were cuddled together on the couch fifteen minutes later, when the baby let out a squawk.

Dani immediately tensed. "I'll go get her."

"Let me." He wanted to test out this theory of his. That he could love another man's child just because it was Dani's. She was flailing her little arms when he got to her, her face scrunched up like she was about to cry.

"Hang on there, Peanut. You shouldn't say a word without your attorney present."

His words seemed to calm her. Gently, he reached his hands under her body, making sure he had a secure hold, then brought her to his chest, blankets and all. He tucked her against his left pec. She sank right into him, like a mini heating pad. Her right cheek was pressed against his body so he could see her face, the button chin, the tiny nose, the dark fluff of hair. So tiny, precious and sweet.

Oh, yes, loving this one was going to be easy, too.

October

FROM THE TOP of the rise, Dani could see the Circle C Ranch spread out before them. She felt a flutter of happiness, mixed with trepidation, and a dash of excitement. Coming home was always a highly emotional affair.

"Impressive," Eliot said. He was in the driver's seat of the SUV they'd rented at the airport in Bozeman. They'd turned off the main road, through the iron gate bearing the Circle C brand, and over the cattle guards that prevented livestock from leaving the property. "How much land did you say your father owns?"

"Pretty much everything you can see from here to the Gallatin Mountains." Dani was sitting in the back, so she could keep an eye on Beverly in her rear-facing, infant traveling seat. It was a big trip for a three-week old infant. The baby had been a dream on the short flight from Seattle. At the airport Dani had nursed her and changed her, and she'd been asleep since the moment they put her in the rented SUV and started driving.

Dani had wished she could bring Mrs. Muddle with them on the trip, but her sisters, Portia and Wren had all promised to help her. She'd learned that when it came to newborns, it really did take a village and holing herself up alone in her condo had really not been a healthy thing to do.

She leaned forward, resting an arm on Eliot's seat, her hand on his shoulder. The aspen had begun to turn, and their gold leaves were dancing in the breeze amid the dark green pines that framed her family home and the outbuildings that surrounded it.

The two-story, Montana-styled log home where she'd grown up was looking in top form for her sister's wedding. A huge white tent had been put up near her mother's old gardens, the outbuildings looked freshly whitewashed, and the grass fields around the home were mowed and trimmed. As they drew nearer they could see barrels of orange and gold chrysanthemums flanking the porch. Sitting on the gliding rocker on the front porch, on look-out duty no doubt, sat her eldest sister Mattie with a man Dani did not recognize.

The day after Mrs. Muddle came into her life, Dani had phoned her sisters and had spoken to them for about an hour each. She'd told them all about her affair with Adrian, her pregnancy and her new daughter. She'd also explained about Eliot. What his friendship had meant to her. And how that friendship had changed into something much deeper. What hadn't been discussed much was the Down Syndrome. She'd touched on it ever so lightly, as if it was a trivial matter. And her sisters had reacted with equal care, not saying much, though she could hear the worry and concern in the tone of their voices.

During her call with Mattie, she'd found out that her older sister had been supported during her split from her husband Wes, by the rancher next door, Nat Diamond. Nat had been a perfect gentleman, Mattie explained, until the divorce was finalized. But since then, she'd discovered that they shared many passions—including one for each other.

Her sister and new beau were standing now, trying to make out who was driving the SUV, no doubt. Since Dani was in the back, and they'd never met Eliot, they were probably confused.

Mattie had said that Nat was good looking—but she hadn't warned Dani to expect a man who looked like Dr. McDreamy on Grey's Anatomy, only taller. "Oh. My. God. He's gorgeous."

"Perhaps," Eliot said. "But probably not nearly as charming or intelligent as the man you're bringing home for the old man's approval."

Dani's light mood immediately darkened. "My father's approval doesn't mean a thing to me. As far as I'm concerned he's just a mean, old goat. I do hope my sisters like you, though."

"Charm the sisters. Check."

Eliot parked the SUV in line with a string of other vehicles including Callan's vintage Dodge truck and their father's rusting blue SUV. Judging by the license plate numbers, Dani guessed the big silver truck was probably Nat Diamond's. She had no idea about the other truck, which looked brand-spanking new.

By now Mattie had figured out who they were and was running to greet them. She had the back door open by the time Dani had the infant car seat unlatched.

"You're here! It's so good to see you! Now, pass me that

baby, I've been dying to meet her."

"She really has," Nat said dryly. "God help us if and when Portia and Wren have children. She's going to be one doting grandmother." He stepped forward to shake Eliot's hand and introduce himself. Dani gave him a brief smile and a hug, but her attention was on her sister. How would she react when she saw Beverly's face?

"Oh, my, she is just the most precious thing. Hold this would you, honey?" Mattie passed the car seat to Nat, who did as requested, keeping it steady as she undid the straps to release the baby.

Beverly's eyes were wide open now as she gazed with interest at her new surroundings. Dani felt herself tensing, waiting for someone to mention the almond-shaped eyes, but all Mattie did was exclaim again how beautiful she was. Only after she'd planted kisses on both of Beverly's cheeks, did she finally turn to Eliot.

"Hi, I'm Mattie. Sorry if I got a little carried away there. We haven't had any babies in this family since my twins were born. And they're in college now."

"Nice to meet you, Mattie. I'm happy to play second fiddle to Beverly anytime."

Mattie's eyes widened when he said the name. She turned to Dani. "You named her after Mom."

"I hope you don't mind." She was worried that her sisters might feel that a less-than-perfect—in some eyes—baby wasn't worthy of their mother's name. But Mattie quelled that silliness with a big hug.

"How perfect. Mom would be so honored."

ROUND ONE WAS over and he was still standing. Eliot shouldered the diaper bag, then grabbed two suitcases, leaving Nat to carry the portable crib. As the two men followed the women toward the house, Eliot noticed Nat was walking with a slight limp.

Dani had explained that he had been recently diagnosed with multiple sclerosis, but other than the limp, Nat seemed strong and perfectly healthy.

"You ready for this?" Dani paused at the large wooden door to ask him.

"Bring it on."

She gave him a brilliant smile, then followed her sister inside.

Eliot's first impression of her family home was of strength and durableness. Heavy wood beams, plank flooring and an impressive river rock fireplace grounded the structure. The furnishings were practical and solid, and the paintings on the walls reflected the natural beauty of the Montana landscape. In her Seattle condo, Dani had created a world for herself that totally removed from this. Her father, Eliot knew, was the reason for that.

And it was also the reason he was interested—if also trepidatious—to meet the man. But the reality was underwhelming. Hawksley Carrigan was seated in a leather arm chair as they entered the family room en masse. He seemed reluctant to set aside his newspaper and rise to greet them. He was shorter than Eliot had expected, with a wiry build and shoulders stooped with age. His thin hair was gray, as was the two-day stubble on his face.

"You're back," was all he said to Dani, clasping her on the shoulder, rather than giving her a hug and a kiss. "I heard you had a baby." But he barely glanced at the bundle in Mattie's hands.

Eliot could tell Dani was relieved that he hadn't taken a closer look. She'd been tensed for a reaction similar to the one she'd had from Adrian. But, it was odd that this man didn't seem even a little interested in his new granddaughter.

"We're naming her Beverly, Dad," Dani said.

His eyes widened at that. If Eliot wasn't mistaken, they even filled with tears. But all he said was, "Good. That's a good choice." He turned to Eliot next. "And you're the lawyer she's taken up with."

He'd made him sound like a flavor of the month, but Eliot didn't object. One day he was going to marry Dani, and this old man would know then that he was in this for the long haul. He shook the man's hand, surprised to find a strong, vice-like grip.

In the dining room off the kitchen they found more family, sitting around a large wooden table and packaging chocolates into small copper-colored boxes.

"Hurray! You're here. We wanted to rush out when we heard your vehicle, but we didn't want to swarm you." Sage was easy to identify, thanks to her red hair. She was pretty, too, but in a completely different way from Dani, or Mattie too, for that matter. She was similar to her sister, however, in the way she bee-lined to the baby. "Oh, let me hold her!"

The good-natured looking cowboy who'd been sitting next to Sage at the table, came around to shake Eliot's hand. "Welcome to the chaos, man."

"I take it you're the lucky groom?" Dawson O'Dell had muscles and a strong, solid build. Eliot knew he was a former rodeo cowboy, but now worked as a county Deputy.

"Sure am. Sage finally said yes. Keep pinching myself in case it's a dream."

"You have to be sleeping to dream, Daddy." A pipsqueak of a girl came up beside him, hair in braids and chocolate smeared at the corners of her mouth. "I'm Savannah. I'm the flower girl. I'm going to wear a dress, and pink cowboy boots. They're really pretty. Want to see them?"

"How about we say hi to your Aunt Dani and the new baby first, Pumpkin?" her father suggested.

"Oh, yeah, I forgot about them." Savannah rushed off, almost tackling Dani with the intensity of her hug.

"She loves the ranch and being part of a big family," Dawson explained. "But she gets a little carried away at times. This wedding has her higher than a kite."

"Dani said something about your mother coming, too? Is she here yet?"

He sighed. "Nope. Patricia will be arriving in the morning with her new boyfriend. Can't wait to meet him," he deadpanned.

"Not too fond of him?"

Dawson shrugged. "Never met him. He's just one in a long string, let's put it that way."

"These chocolates look wonderful," Dani said. "Can we

sample?"

"Only the broken ones," Savannah piped up. "But I'm good at breaking them, so there's lots over here." She pointed to where she'd been sitting.

"You have to try my sister's chocolates," Dani fed him one of the rich-looking morsels. "These are her famous salty caramels."

"Coated in seventy-percent, single origin chocolate," Sage added.

Eliot nodded, showing his approval.

"The chocolate are delicious, but have you had dinner?" Mattie asked. "We can offer pulled pork sandwiches and coleslaw."

Dani's eyes brightened. "Is it Grandma Brambles' recipe?"

"Absolutely."

Dani tucked her hand around his arm and pulled him into the kitchen. "You have to try this. It's the best coleslaw in the world."

He didn't need to be convinced. He was hungry and the pulled pork sounded pretty tempting, too.

"Beer?" Dawson asked.

"Absolutely. A lager if you have one."

"Sure thing. We're well stocked for the weekend." Dawson winked, as he pulled open a gigantic fridge.

Everything in this kitchen was huge, from the large island at the center, to the cast iron range and the industrial-sized dishwasher. Eliot could tell this was the room where the Carrigan girls spent the most time and felt most at home.

They'd probably spent a lot of time with their mother in here.

He and Dani sat at the island to eat their meals, which were every bit as delicious as promised. When he was done, he counted heads and realized he still hadn't met everyone. "Where's Callan? And the twins?"

"Out in the barn doing evening chores," Mattie said. "They should be in soon. It's almost dark." Turning to Dani she added, "I can't believe Portia kept your secret for so long. The little minx."

Along with the others, Eliot gazed out the west-facing windows. The sun had already dipped below the Gallatin Range and the mountains were glowing with a faint purple haze.

"Sure is pretty out here," he said, thinking of the painting Dani kept in her study. Despite her complicated feelings about her father, she loved Montana and now he understood why.

"It is," Dani said. "How about we go out to the barns and see if we can find those girls?"

Eliot nodded. It would feel good to stretch his legs. After checking with Sage and Mattie to make sure they were okay being left with Beverly for a while, he and Dani went out the back door, following a stone path that curved around the gardens and the area with the tent, beyond a bunch of shrubs and trees, to the barns and corrals. But they didn't need to go any further, because three cowgirls were walking toward them and Eliot honestly couldn't tell which one was Dani's baby sister and which were Mattie's twins. They were all wearing jeans and western shirts, dirty cowboy boots and hats. They still hadn't spotted them and were talking quietly among themselves. The slightly taller one on the left said something and the others laughed.

And then the shortest, curviest girl glanced up in their direction, paused, and then exclaimed. "It's them! They're here!"

"Hey there, Portia!" Dani wrapped her niece in a big hug. "I'd like you to meet Eliot."

"Where's the baby?"

Eliot was getting used to that question and it made him glad. Nothing meant more to Dani than having her daughter loved unconditionally by her family.

He met the other twin, next. Wren was quieter than Portia, with thoughtful, intelligent eyes and a slimmer build, rather like her aunt. Callan had a slim, petite frame and an extremely pretty, heart-shaped face. Despite her small size, she had a man-sized grip and shook Eliot's hand before she relented and gave him a tentative hug.

"So you're a lawyer, huh?"

"I am."

She planted her fists on her slim hips. "And you've known my sister how long?"

"We've lived next door to each other for a few years now." Eliot tried not to laugh. He was finally getting the grilling most guys would expect from their girlfriend's father. This Callan was quite the tough lady. He'd do well not to cross her.

ON THE MORNING of Sage's wedding, Dani was up early breastfeeding Beverly on the porch when Sage joined her. She had a cup of coffee and put another on the table for Dani.

"Decaf," she assured her, before sitting on one of the wicker chairs and leaning back with a sigh. "What a beautiful morning."

"I'm glad. I hope everything about today is perfect for you."

"My family is here and I get to marry the man I've been in love with for years, complete with the cutest little step-daughter. Anything more is just icing. And I'm talking fondant, obviously."

Dani smiled. "At least something good came out of your barrel racing. You wouldn't have met Dawson if dad hadn't practically forced you to take up the sport."

"I don't regret it now, though I did hate it back then. Not the practicing, I loved that. It was performing that made me sick." Sage took a sip of her coffee. Her beautiful hair was wet from the shower. Later Portia was going to curl it for her. Sage had pooh-poohed the idea of a beauty salon appointment, said she'd prefer to spend a relaxing day with the family instead.

Beverly let out a little burp, and Dani pulled her up, sitting her on her knee and rubbing the baby's back to give her stomach a chance to settle.

"She's such a sweet baby," Sage said. "Dani, why didn't

tell us that you were pregnant?"

"I've been thinking about that," Dani admitted. "I guess it goes back to how my role in the family changed when Mom died. Mattie was already married, with children of her own. That left me in charge of you and Callan."

"Dad certainly wasn't much help," Sage agreed.

"I wouldn't say I stopped being your sister and suddenly became your mother. But I did have to step up in a lot of areas. Dad hired a housekeeper, but I made your lunches and checked that you ate breakfast and brushed your teeth. I helped with homework and looked after you when you were sick."

"You're right. You did so much. And none of us ever thanked you."

Dani waved a hand. "I'm sure at the time you found me bossy and overbearing. But I didn't enjoy being the bad guy all the time either. Plus, Dad and I butt heads a lot back then. So, by the time I'd finished high school I was pretty desperate for my freedom."

"No wonder you left Montana. But it makes me sad that when you needed help, you didn't feel you could call any of us."

"I was afraid you'd tell me something I didn't want to hear. Like, I was a fool to have a baby on my own. Or that I should go for more testing when the ultrasound tech told me my baby was showing markers for Downs."

"Well." Sage reached over to play with the little fingers on one of Beverly's hands. "Just like my barrel racing days, it looks like the last nine months have paid off for you, too.

Not only do you have this sweet girl, but I have to say, I really like Eliot and so does Dawson."

"Thanks Sage. It means a lot to hear you say that."

The sisters hugged, and when Sage pulled back she said, "Please, next time life throws you a curveball—call me?"

"I promise."

With perfect timing, Beverly squawked, demanding more food, and after Dani moved her to the other breast she noticed a vehicle approaching from the highway.

"Oh! My flowers!" Sage jumped up from her chair and went to great the newcomer.

Dani had walked by the new SweetPea Flowers shop in Marietta a few times, since the new shop was next door to Sage's Copper Mountain Chocolates, but she'd never met the owner. She pulled a blanket over the baby and smiled as Sage brought Risa Davison up on the porch to say hello.

Risa's dark curly hair was pulled back into a ponytail and she was carrying an exquisite bouquet of baby yellow roses surrounding a pale, pink calla lily. "So nice to meet you, Dani. And congratulations on your new baby. Must be busy, huh?"

"Yes. But in a good way."

"I'll bet. May I see her?"

Beverly had unlatched from her breast, so Dani made a few quick adjustments, then pulled aside the blanket.

"Aw. She's adorable." Risa seemed utterly unfazed by the almond-shaped eyes that had turned toward her at the sound of her voice. "You're so lucky."

Dani knew that Risa had recently married former Marine, Monty Davison, and they were now living out on the Red Barn. Maybe they were hoping to start a family, too? But whether that was true, or not, the very fact that Risa would call her lucky, warmed Dani's heart.

She did feel lucky. With each day that passed she loved her daughter more, and felt so blessed to have her in her life. And Eliot. He was the rock she'd thought she'd never find. Just seeing how easily he'd fit into her Montana family had cemented her belief in him and their budding new relationship.

They were friends, on the verge of becoming lovers. And Dani couldn't wait. But first there was this wedding, Sage's special day. She wanted to help make sure that everything was perfect.

And it was. Sage's best friends Jenny, Selah, and Chelsea were there as well as the gorgeous new men in their lives. Jenny, pregnant and glowing, Chelsea with a sparkly new diamond from her very rich and sexy new fiancé.

Despite the fact that they were their nearest neighbors, none of the Sheenan boys came, out of deference to Hawksley and his life-long feud with their father.

Grouchy Great-Aunt Mabel was there, however, along with her great niece, Eliza Bramble. Eliza ran a bed and breakfast in the historic Bramble family house in Marietta. Dani made sure to introduce her daughter and Eliot to both Great-Aunt Mabel and Eliza. It seemed unfortunate to her that though their cousin had moved to Marietta from

Nashville a few years ago, and was close in age to Sage, none of them knew Eliza very well.

At one time, Dani had been suspicious that Eliza might be after whatever remained of the Bramble's copper mining fortune. But today, she was feeling magnanimous and put her cousin's reticence down to shyness.

The one false note in the day was when Hawksley walked Sage down the aisle. He stumbled a bit after handing Sage's arm to Dawson, then almost collapsed, before Sage and Dawson intervened and helped him to his chair. A glass of water had seemed to revive him, but Dani thought his complexion was still a little grey. If only he would agree to go to the doctor. But, stubbornly, he insisted he was fine.

And he probably was. The ornery old coot would probably live to one hundred.

Dinner and toasts were over, and people were dancing to the lively bluegrass music being played on a raised platform in the tent. Dani looked for Eliot and found him heading for her.

"I just put Beverly down to sleep. Several women are chatting in the kitchen, and they promised to keep an eye on her."

God he looked good, elegant and handsome in his beautiful charcoal suit. A lot of the men were dressed in Western wear today, but Eliot managed to look perfectly comfortable and at ease among them. He had a gift for mingling with people, Dani realized. It came from being the sort of person who cared about others and didn't spend too much time fussing about himself.

"I want to dance with the most beautiful woman on the Circle C Ranch." Eliot held out his arm, and she gladly took it. She'd grown up on this ranch. But in Eliot's arms she was truly home.

The End

Excerpt from Snowbound in Montana

ADORNED IN CHRISTMAS finery, the Bramble House Bed and Breakfast had never looked better, while Eliza Bramble, manager and great-niece of the owner, had never felt worse. If she had guessed that her blog post on decorating for the holidays would go viral, she would never have hit the "Publish" button.

But she had. And since she couldn't turn back time for a do-over, she was going to have to come up with a Plan B for the holidays. A plan that would get her out of Marietta, Montana until Christmas was over.

She had one figured out, already. The tricky part would be explaining her departure to her Great Aunt Mable. Mable was not the sort to embrace change at the best of times. And Christmas, for their family, was never the best of times.

They were seated in the breakfast room of Bramble House, at the large, linen-covered table that could accommodate twelve with comfort. When it was just the two of them, like today, Mable took the chair at the head of the table overlooking the east-facing windows, while Eliza sat to her right.

On the table was a pot of English Breakfast tea, the matching china creamer and sugar bowl, and a ramekin of strawberry preserves. At each place setting were two slices of crispy toast, a small dish of fruit salad, and a tea cup. Cutlery was laid out on linen napkins that had been in the Bramble family for over fifty years—purchased along with many other linens, two china sets, and the silver, by Mable's parents on their wedding trip abroad to France and England in 1925. It was not the china they set out when they had paying guests. For that they used second-hand pieces Eliza had painstakingly located and purchased on e-Bay.

Aunt Mable had a disconcerting resemblance to the Dowager Countess on her favorite TV series, Downton Abbey: swept-up gray hair, prissy mouth, and laser-sharp blue eyes. Eyes that were currently focused on Eliza with distressing sharpness.

"What do you mean you want to go away for Christmas?" Mable's gaze shifted briefly to the Christmas tree in the far corner of the room. This year Eliza had decorated trees for all the downstairs main rooms, each with a theme drawn from the Bramble family's past. The tree in the breakfast room had ornaments made of copper, with gold and silver accents, representing their mining history.

"My reasons are personal, Aunt Mable. I'm afraid I can't say more."

"But we're fully booked for the holidays, aren't we?"

"Yes. I've asked my sister and her husband to stand in for me. They'll prepare the breakfasts and afternoon teas." Other meals were not included, guests were expected to make reservations in one of the many restaurants and cafes Marietta had to offer.

"Caroline and Frank?"

"Yes." It had taken a lot to convince them. They'd been planning to go to Maui for the holidays—their usual method of escaping the holiday madness. Eliza's two brothers likewise had booked tropical destinations for Christmas, as had her parents. They were not the sort of family who went for the traditional turkey, tree and gift exchange sort of thing.

"But you made such an effort this year. All your baking and decorating—" Mable waved a hand to indicate not only the tree in the corner, but the cedar boughs on the fireplace mantle, the cranberry candles at the center of the table, and the fairy lights sparkling like stars on the mullioned windows.

"I had to do something to attract bookings. We almost broke even this year. I'm hoping we'll finally get the accounts in the black this December."

"Yes. I understand all that. What puzzles me is why, after all your hard work, and knowing how important the next week will be for our bottom line, as you like to call it, you would just want to take off and go on a holiday. It doesn't make sense."

Eliza smeared a spoonful of preserves on her toast. "Do you remember when I first moved into Bramble House?"

It had been two years ago. She'd shown up on her aunt's door with two suitcases and her purse, asking her aunt if she could turn the ancestral home into a bed and breakfast. She'd heard, through the family e-mail loop that Mable was thinking of selling—she could no longer afford the upkeep and property taxes on the big, old house.

But Mable had really wanted to keep her home and she'd leapt at Eliza's offer.

"If you hadn't shown up that day, I'd probably be living in one of those awful condos for seniors by now."

"But do you remember what I looked like? The shape I was in?"

"You were dreadfully skinny, with that awful fake brown hair. And sad. Sometimes, at night I would hear you crying in your room."

This was the first Eliza had heard of that, and the news made her smile ruefully. Some aunts might have tapped on her door and offered help—a pot of tea and a wee chat, perhaps?

But Mable was not that sort of aunt.

"Someone hurt me, badly. And I think he might be about to do it again. That's why I have to go. I'm really sorry if you feel like I'm abandoning you and Bramble House for the holidays. But I simply don't have any choice."

❧ ❦

ELIZA CLIMBED UP the stairs to the store front of the Montana Wilds Adventure Company. A huge window display depicted a cozy scene right out of a ski chalet. Two mannequins, dressed in Norwegian sweaters and ski pants, lounged before a cast iron stove. Artfully arranged around them were sets of skis, poles, boots and all the accessories that went with them. In the background was a Scotch pine, decorated for Christmas with sporty wooden ornaments including tiny wooden sleds and miniature ice skates.

When she pulled open the heavy door, the aroma of hot apple and cinnamon cider and the familiar refrain from the Little Drummer Boy, completed the Christmas presentation. Last minute shoppers were everywhere, purchasing mittens, hats and other stocking stuffers, she supposed. A small queue waited at the cash register, where a young woman with her hair in braids seemed to be dealing with them with cheerful competence.

Eliza scanned the busy room, looking for someone to help her. A man who looked to be in his late forties, with a thin face and wearing a plaid flannel shirt gave her a nod and was soon beside her.

"Can I help you find something?"

"I want to sign up for the Nordic Holiday Package. The one for five days, December twenty-second to the twenty-sixth. I saw it on your website, but when I tried to register I got a message, *page not found.*"

"That's because it's full-up. Sorry, I've asked my wife, Gracie to fix that—she updates our website, but I guess she's fallen behind. Marshall!" He called out to a tall man who'd just emerged from the back, cell phone pressed to one ear. "That's Marshall McKenzie," he explained to Eliza. "He's the one leading the group." Raising his voice again, he called out, "The Nordic Holiday Package is full, right?"

The man named Marshall held up his hand for them to wait while he finished his call. He made a note in an open binder on a back counter, then walked toward them.

He was in his thirties like her, tall, with a lean, athletic build and a plain, but pleasant face.

"It's been full for weeks, Ryan." Marshall's gaze shifted from the bearded man to Eliza. He had warm brown eyes and an open smile. "Are you the one inquiring?"

"Yes. I'm Eliza Bramble. My plans for Christmas changed unexpectedly and I was really hoping to get away for a few days."

"You do realize the trip leaves tomorrow? It's been sold out for over a month."

The man with the thin face left to assist another customer and now it was just the two of them, standing in front of a rack of the Norwegian sweaters on display in the front window.

"I know this is last minute. But I love cross country skiing. And I really don't want to be in town for the holidays this year." She smiled and shrugged, sensing Marshall might be convinced to help her, if he possibly could. He had the air of someone who liked helping people. The kind of nice, young man that women ought to fall in love with…but so rarely did.

"How many in your party?"

It took her a second to understand what he was asking. "Oh. Just me."

Marshall took a moment to mull that over. "Maybe you'd consider our New Year's Eve Backcountry Adventure? We have mostly singles signed up for that one, and still have space for a few more."

"It has to be Christmas," she insisted.

"Well, I might be able to squeeze another room out of

Griff. He and his wife Betsy own the Baker Creek Lodge where we'll be staying. But I'm afraid it wouldn't have a fireplace like the others. Also, I think it's too late to include any of your gifts on the Santa sleigh."

She'd read about that. Guests could arrange to have their Christmas gifts delivered to the lodge by Santa driving a horse drawn sleigh. "I don't mind either of those things."

"Yes, well the Santa thing is more popular with our families who have children. We have two of them in this group, as well as two couples without children. One set is in their fifties, the other in their thirties. It probably won't be the most exciting group for you."

"I won't mind," she insisted.

"The agenda is pretty simple. Breakfast will be provided, along with bagged lunches. We ski all day, then break for afternoon tea in the lodge. After dinner, people sometimes play board games by the fire, or just sit and read. We'll have a fondue and steak dinner Christmas Eve, brunch on Christmas morning and a roast turkey with all the trimmings that evening. But other than that, it'll be pretty low key."

"Sounds perfect."

"You sure?"

She could see the questions in his eyes. Why didn't she want to spend the holidays with her family? Was there some sort of problem? Possibly with her?

"I am sure. I brought cash," she added, pulling out her wallet.

Marshall laughed. "Ryan loves cash. I think we've got a deal."

She started toward the line-up at the front but Marshall stopped her. "I can take care of this for you." He led her toward the back counter where there was a second register, as well as the binder he'd been writing in earlier.

As he rang up her receipt, she noticed a display of toques. A gray one with a red snowflake design on the front caught her eye. "Would you add this, please?"

"Sure thing." He finished the transaction, made a note in the binder, then passed her a receipt. "You're set now. You'll love the network of trails in the Deerlodge National Forest. Something for everyone. You've been skiing about two years now, right?"

Yes. She'd taken up the sport her first winter in Marietta and had been thrilled by how quickly she'd caught on. "How did you know?"

"I sold you your skis. You told me you'd never tried Nordic skiing before and I promised you'd love it."

A vague memory surfaced. A confusing array of skis, boots and poles, and then one polite man helping her choose exactly the right things. "I *do* remember." She hesitated, feeling a little embarrassed. "I'm sorry I didn't recognize you."

"Oh, no worries. It was two years ago." He handed her receipt and smiled again. "You changed your hair color."

"Yes. This is my natural color. The other was just...an experiment." She'd dyed her hair brown when she'd left Nashville for Marietta, so broken hearted she'd wanted to be a different person. Only recently had she decided to go back to her original color. If she'd known what was about to happen with her blog, she would have remained a brunette.

"See you tomorrow. We catch the bus here, at eight in the morning."

She left the shop, still feeling badly. Yes, it had been two years ago. But he'd managed to remember *her*. Even with her new hair color.

☙ ❧

MARSHALL PUT AWAY the trip binder, trying to decide if it would be better to notify Griff and Betsy about the extra booking by phone or email. Since they couldn't yell at him by email, he decided on the latter. As he typed out the message on the store computer, he found himself humming along to the carol playing over the sound system.

He didn't know why he was suddenly in such a good mood. Or why he was going out of his way to make room for Eliza Bramble on this trip. Sure, she was pretty. He'd thought so the first time he'd seen her. But with her blonde hair—which suited her fair skin and glowing caramel eyes better than the brown had—she was now even lovelier. Not that it mattered. A gorgeous woman like that was definitely out of his league.

Marshall didn't have much luck with the fairer sex, despite meeting a lot of them in his line of work. Most trips he'd end up with at least one of the female guests giving him her number. But it never worked out. Attempts at dating were awkward. They never seemed to click.

It bothered him sometimes, his bad luck with women. But he wasn't lonely, or unhappy. He had a job he loved and lots of friends, both male and female.

"You're too nice, Marshall. Women like a bad boy."

He got that line a lot. Which mystified him to no end. Did women really like bad boys? His inability to understand why, was, he suspected, the key to his lack of success in the romance department.

When he was finished with the final preparations for tomorrow's trip, he checked in with Ryan. "I'm heading off now. I'll be back to work on the twenty-seventh."

"Have a good trip. The blonde going with you?"

Marshall nodded.

"I figured you'd find a way to squeeze her in." Ryan winked. "In your shoes, I would have, too. Before you go, check my desk in the back. There's an envelope with your name—that's your Christmas bonus. And a package, too. UPS delivered it while you were on your lunch break. Forgot to mention it sooner."

Marshall thanked him for the bonus, wished him a Merry Christmas, then went to the back where he peeked at the size of the check before sliding it into his back pocket. The package turned out to be what he'd expected. About the size of shoe box, with a return address from Albany, New York.

He exited out the back way, stopping at the bank to deposit his bonus, before continuing to the little clapboard he rented, just a few blocks off Main Street.

Once inside, he ripped open the box, read the Christmas card from his mother, step-father and two half-sisters, then took a bite of one of the chocolate chip cookies.

He didn't know why his mother continued to send him

two dozen home-made cookies every Christmas. The cost of the postage was probably double the value of the cookies themselves. Was it to remind him that he had a family and that he was loved? Or was it a salve to her guilt, to the way she'd gone on to build a new family after their old one imploded?

Marshall honestly didn't know the answer. He only wished she'd stop sending the cookies. They'd been his brother Dean's favorites and they always made him feel a little sad.

⌒ ⌒

AFTER SUCCESSFULLY BOOKING her ski trip, Eliza stopped at Copper Mountain Chocolates. She'd already finished her Christmas shopping—gift cards for Jo and Ella, who did the cleaning and laundry at Bramble House, and a beautiful wool shawl for her Aunt Mable. But she needed to pick up something for her sister and brother-in-law. Her family didn't usually do gifts, but given the favor Caro and Frank were doing for her this year, Eliza felt she had to buy them something.

Gourmet chocolates seemed like a safe choice. Still, Eliza hesitated a moment before pushing open the door.

The shop owner, Sage Carrigan, was Eliza's cousin. Sage had three sisters, another of whom, Callan, lived in the Marietta area. Eliza wanted to be close with these girls, who were all around her age, but she'd started on the wrong foot when she'd first moved to town. She'd been so miserable when she'd first arrived in town that she'd spurned both

Sage, and her younger sister Callan's, friendly overtures, going so far as to make up a story about a bereavement.

When she'd opened up Bramble House as a bed and breakfast, she knew there were suspicions that she was somehow taking advantage of Aunt Mable. Which was a laugh. If there'd ever been a great Bramble fortune, it was long gone now. She'd seen her aunt's bank accounts. The poor woman was barely scraping by—something Eliza hoped to remedy once Bramble House was operating to its potential.

Then, this summer when she'd asked for assess to their late mother's diaries for the family history she was working on, the Carrigans had refused her access.

Eliza knew it wasn't fair to blame her cousins—Sage, Callan or the other sisters, Dani and Mattie. She was pretty sure it was the father, Hawksley Carrigan, who was being so stubborn. Still, the refusal had hurt.

But lately Sage had made a few encouraging overtures, including inviting Eliza to her wedding this past October. So—she should stop being silly and go inside and buy those gifts she needed.

The chocolate shop was bustling, so packed with customers Eliza could hardly move. And no wonder—Sage was handing out small samples of her molten hot cocoa. Even with her red hair pulled back into a long braid, and wearing a simple apron with the store logo on the front, Sage looked beautiful.

She smiled at Eliza, as she handed her a paper cup of cocoa. "So nice to see you, Eliza. How is Aunt Mable?"

Earlier in the year Mable had been taken to emergency after a fall. "She's well, thankfully."

"Glad to hear it. Sounds like you're going to have a full house for Christmas. I can't believe your blog, Eliza! It's wonderful! Dawson and I saw you on TV, too. Can you believe how much press you're getting?"

"It's more than I counted on," Eliza admitted. "It's been overwhelming. The website actually crashed at one point, we had so many hits."

"The themed Christmas trees are brilliant. I love that you made each one reflect a different aspect of the Bramble family."

Eliza had indulged her inner child with not just the mining-themed tree in the breakfast room, but also a literary-themed tree in the library, a Bramble tree in the sitting room, a baking tree in the kitchen and a huge thirteen foot Montana-themed tree in the foyer.

"The recipes are popular, too." Eliza had gone through all the old cookbooks in the Bramble House kitchen. It seemed nothing had ever been thrown away. Some of the recipes dated back to the eighteen hundreds, when the Brambles first settled in Marietta. She'd selected recipes to suit a Christmas menu, tested them, then posted them on the Bramble House Blog, along with her decorating tips.

"I bet they are. Lots of them were favorites of my mother's." Sage's expression grew wistful, even though it had been almost two decades since she and her sisters had lost their mother in a ranching accident.

Eliza struggled to find the right thing to say—something

tactful that didn't involve the diaries—but before she had a chance, the woman in line behind her, said politely, "Excuse me, but we've been waiting a long time back here for a sample of that cocoa."

"Of course." Sage gave Eliza an apologetic smile, then continued handing samples to her other customers.

Eliza moved on, picking out an attractive box of assorted chocolates for her sister, then waiting patiently in line to pay for her purchase. She was ready to leave, when Sage once more called out her name.

"Eliza! You can't leave without confirming the story. Is John Urban really coming to Marietta for the Christmas holidays?"

Eliza froze.

"I mean, he's just so *hot*. And that voice! This town will go crazy if he actually shows up. But he's such a big country music star. It was just a publicity stunt, right?"

Eliza wished some more customers would show up, demanding samples of rich cocoa. But several groups had just left the store, and at that moment, there was only Sage and her two employees, all of whom were staring at her.

"H-he is booked in," Eliza confirmed.

"Wow," said the young woman at the cash register. "I wish he'd give us a concert. Wouldn't it be neat if he teamed up with Landry Bell?"

"Oh, yes," said the other employee, a very thin woman who was restocking one of the displays. "And Rayanne Grey could open for them." To Eliza, she explained, "Rayanne is a local girl, still looking for her big break. Landry bought one of her songs a while ago."

"That does sound like a dream concert," Eliza agreed. "But I wouldn't count on it ever happening."

"I wonder what the draw for John Urban is," Sage mulled. "I mean, why would someone like that, who isn't married and doesn't have children, want to leave Nashville and come to small town Marietta for Christmas?"

"I can't imagine," Eliza murmured. And before they could ask another question, she rushed out the door.

Find out what happens next in *Snowbound in Montana*

The Carrigans of Circle C

Hawksley Carrigan, owner of the Circle C Ranch south of Marietta, Montana, always wanted a son to carry on the family name. Unfortunately for him, he ended up with four daughters

Book 1: Promise Me, Cowboy

Sage Carrigan's story

Book 2: Good Together

Mattie Carrigan's story

Book 3: Close to Her Heart

Dani Carrigan's story

Book 4: Snowbound in Montana

Eliza Bramble's story

Book 5: A Cowgirl's Christmas

Callan Carrigan's story

About the Author

Hard to imagine a more glamorous life than being an accountant, isn't it? Still, I gave up the thrills of income tax forms and double entry book-keeping when I sold my first book in 1998. Hard to believe I've now written more than 40 (2 of which were nominated for RITAs).

When I'm not writing I love to be out hiking, cross-country skiing or biking. I'm not athletic—I just enjoy the outdoors, especially here in Calgary, where I live, and on Flathead Lake, Montana, where we have a cottage. My partner Mike and I share this in common. We also love to play cribbage and Scrabble. If a glass of wine is on the table, so much the better!

Visit C.J.'s website at CJCarmichael.com

Made in the USA
Columbia, SC
21 September 2023